ALL THINGS *Chorus*

ALL THINGS *Chorus*

(A Novel)

By: *Anne Wien Lynn*

iUniverse, Inc.
Bloomington

All Things Chorus

iUniverse books may be ordered through booksellers or by contacting:

iUniverse
1663 Liberty Drive
Bloomington, IN 47403
www.iuniverse.com
1-800-Authors (1-800-288-4677)

ISBN: 978-1-4759-5946-8 (sc)
ISBN: 978-1-4759-5947-5 (ebk)

Printed in the United States of America

iUniverse rev. date: 01/04/2013

CONTENTS

Love, the best gift in the world;
Love, the only gift in the world;
Love, the reason God created all things;
Love, the source of all lives;
Love, the best education in the world;
Love, the basic education in the world;
Love, makes human been;
Love, makes us to close to God.

All Things Bright and Beautiful,
All Creatures Great and Small,
All Things Wise and Wonderful,
——Cecil Frances Alexander

Sun, moon, stars, clouds, mountains, thunder, lightning, oceans, rivers, rain, rainbow, all trees, flowers, each leaf, every path, every elf, all birds, beasts, fishes and insects, all human beings, all gods, all of God's creation, everything in the universe is going to be harmonious under God's baton . . . .

1

The Global Village Of Music

Sitting alone in the blue long chair in the terminal, Jin was staring at the busy airport out of the big bright wall windows, and those deferent size aircraft. Ark twelve-year-old boy was sitting by her, using earphone listening to the music. Jin's sister Medie and five girls were sleeping on the sits. They came from Beijing, right now, it was midnight there. Sky was blue, Jin's mood was somber. They were just passing the city Vancouver, landing, transit airplane, need total four hours, their destination was Toronto.

Ark closed his eyes, he was tired too after the long time flight. But Jin saw that his arms began to wave, strong rhythms, distinctive melody line, the boy started to "conduct" by the music, but eyes were still closed, his frame looked very professional just liked Kara Jan, attracted some past travelers curious gathered to watch him.

Jin was watching every of his small action. Ark wore a white T-shirt, printed "Noah Ark", his fluffy bright and tidy hair was trembling by his body in the music. But no body could hear the music.

At this moment, two tall thin white men who looked about 30-year-old carrying travel bags came to Ark, they stood in front of him, and followed his conduct gesture, one made action to "knocking drum", other one "pretend trumpets". But Jin saw what they were playing was right the pilgrims chorus in Wagner's opera "Tannhauser: Pilgrims Chorus" by Ark's conduction, they undoubtedly were professional musicians, they were able to see the silent music from Ark' conduct. It was really a unexpected encounter!

The silent music performances attracted more viewers stop to watch them in curious and smiled. When the end of the sound, Ark bared his right hand, made a clean and beautiful arc in the air. Applause was around him startled, Ark opened his eyes, and looked around in surprise, there were so many people behind him. Two white men applause to Ark too, smiled and stepped forward casually touched Ark's hair, one took out a business card to Jin, then they both were backward, chic ground saluted to Ark said: "See you! Captain." (meant Ark was the captain of the Noah's Ark) Then they turn to run away.

Ark didn't not know what happened, he touched his head. Jin smiled to him, raised her cell phone camcorder to show him, and the business card. Ark took over, read it in English:

"Los Angeles Philharmonic Orchestra, percussion Minister, Daniel Davis. Wow!"

2

LOVE—MAKES US CLOSE TO GOD

The big auditorium of Toronto Englewood college could accommodate three thousand people where was Trinity Christian Church meeting place on every Sunday. Today was a special day, Dean leads everybody sing priest first, then pray, pastor John sermons for an hour entitled "It's more blessed to give than to receive."

After sermon, pastor John announced that we had a brother and sister, Malaysia Chinese, married but no kid for many years, they decided to go to Shanghai, China, adopt an orphan, they were leaving tomorrow. Pastor John hopes that everyone here pray for them, Lord blessed them, gave them peace on the way, also brought his love to this new family.

In the final pray and thanksgiving, the routine programs of church activities had ended, but after the break, everyone returned to the seat, and soon calm down, they were looking forward to the next special program.

The red curtain on the stage was pulled, which causes everyone's curiosity, because it was rare in the past. The electronic big screens at both sides of the stage show out the text:

"Please keep quiet, thank you!"

All the lights were off on the auditorium, the stage lights were dim, became faint blue, when all audience were quiet liked empty, people felt a soft breath came with light winds from the edge of sky, mountains and lake shore, the moon, and in that breeze to fill the gap of silence, a voice was from a night of pure lake, rising from the blue water slowly, hazy mist, fog, moonlight as bright and clean, and slightly elegant with a trace of sadness. Gradually, the other slightly deep voice came into the more voices have joined quietly express a richer and more profound level, background and more distinct topics.

This sound liked telling a remote beautiful legends, under the shinning moonlight, the quiet lake liked a dark blue satin, rippled from a holy and lonely life center to the surrounding layers, silently, go in to people's dreams. A fairy lives away from the hubbub in the night of the lake, was quiet, the free to open herself, slowly, silently swim in the mist drifting in the lake, takes the shower of moonlight.

The thousands years moonlight, thousands years lakes, thousands years music, made every one shower in the vast night of freedom in the glory, their hearts became so pure, sublimated, so that they could not help but want to deeply sincerely worship to the moonlight witch was the music brought to them.

Saint-Saens' Cello song "Swan", a lot of people were very familiar, but used voice to sing, it was the first time people heard it. When the music fell down, the host Dean came back to the stage.

Applause. Dean stood in front of the altar by the side of the stage, looking around the audience, convinced that all eyes were on to him, he has always been calm and clear to start the voice said:

"Sincerely thanks Lord, so let us enjoy the wonderful sounds of holy now, maybe a lot of people want to know where this voice come from? At this moment, I think of Jessie sister, she has told me that when she first came to our church, many people saw her, all took the initiative to say hello to her and asked her name, introduced themselves, shook hands with her very warmly and sincerely to welcome her joined our church. Jessie said that day she was very touched, because she had never been shook hands with so many people, so that day the last, her hands were numb."

The audience laughed, some people applauded. Dean continued: "In order to avoid some body's hand got numb again," he stopped, knowing the audience, and applause, Dean smiled and nodded, "Thanks Lord! Yes, there are new friends to our church today. In the past, whenever some new friends to join, everyone here was very happy. warmly welcome them, our Trinity Church, in the past twenty years, grown up from the first three individuals to now more than 3,000 sisters and brothers."

The audience again applauded.

"Praise the Lord!" Dean continued, "Really, I do think for a long time, that in what way, to introduce our new friends to you all, because they are really special. Until a day one week ago, at my ESL class, a friend told me a story, this story gave me a great inspiration. The friend said: once upon ago, in a salon in Paris, was already very famous musicians Liszt and writers George Sand invited friends to a piano concert, but they said that they wanted to temporarily extinguished all the candles, made everyone enjoyed in the dark due to see nothing. So, everyone listened carefully the music, whether it's beautiful melodies, poetic musical language, as well as its extraordinary musical skills, have conquered the audience's heart deeply. music was still buzzing at the end, it was like crazy drunk, after that, George Sand hold candles came out from behind the curtain, she put the candlesticks on the piano, candlelight face of the young musicians. In this manner, George Sand and Liszt introduced the unremarkable Polish musician Chopin to the Paris high society people through his music, knowledge and understanding of him and accepted his talent. Perhaps, have any brothers and sisters here also seen the movie? Yes, the movie called <<A Sound For Remember>>. Now, please allow me in the same way, to introduce our new friends to you. They are—'Philharmonic girls cappella vocal chorus'!"

The curtains was opened, people finally saw the five Chinese girls on the stage, the oldest one looks like 15-year-old, the youngest one was about 11-year-old, they're all wearing white dress, blue ribbon on their waist and head. The five girls can be said that no one looks beautiful, however, their faces are peaceful, white skin, calm demeanor, temperament extraordinary, causing all of the church's interest, especially their superb singing skills so much.

Applause resounded through the hall, the girls collectively bowed to the audience. Dean nodded and said: "Well, now please allow me to introduce to you: Philharmonic Girls chorus is from Beijing China with their teacher that they had just immigrated to Canada, came to Toronto witch the city has the most races in the world, I'd like to tell every body that these five kids are all orphans, they lost their family and their school when earthquake in Sichuan province in China. Seven years ago, two ladies have adopted them, so, this is a very special family. Before coming to Canada, they lived in Beijing, and they were members of China National Symphony Orchestra Children And Young Women Chorus, this chorus has repeatedly visited many countries, such as Australia, Hong Kong, Taiwan, Singapore, Japan, Russia, Italy, Austria, Monaco, U.S. etc., they sung a lot of Chinese and foreign art songs, folk songs and classical repertoire. They also participated in some of the performances of the opera, such as "Turandot", "career as an artist," Tosca "and" Carmen ", they also participated in the opening ceremony of the Beijing 2008 Olympic Games. They are world-class level, won many awards. Austrian Chancellor had given them high marks, President Reagan had also signed the highest appreciation for their certificate. Philharmonic girls chorus has published two sets of CDs and DVDs. Our brothers and sisters here who love classical music may know some other well-known contemporary a cappella vocal chorus, such as The King' Singers, the Swingle Singers, Celtic Woman and All Angeles, etc. You do not know the Lunar Philharmonic girl groups, because they are too young, still in growth stage. I invited them today to be here, because, as new immigrants to Canada, Canada's fresh blood, they need our help now, the main source of their income is from their mother's hard labor jobs and the welfare of government, not enough to support their music career, they want through their own efforts to show their talent, strong more friends, more people know our church is large, so many brothers and sisters here do different jobs. I hope you are willing to help them, for example, help them find music agents, recording new CD and DVD, looking for a professional rehearsal place, contact the performances, etc. etc. Of course, we first need to fully understand them. A month ago, my wife Ella and me, invited sisters Jessie, visited this special family. The five girls have very special names, they were called Gong, Shang, Jiao, Zhi and Yu. We do not know what these mean, their mom said that these represent the five strings on the Chinese Guqin."

Dean went on to say: "Now, before my brothers and sisters dedicate your love, you certainly hope for this with love and music composed to build more understanding of the special family. So, I propose, we can ask questions in this free on issues of interest to you, ask anyone who they were. Jessie sisters here, to translate for everyone now, please."

Applause, Jessie came to stage by girls. Some people raised their hands, the clergy immediately sent over the wireless microphone.

A tall black brother stood up, he said: "May I ask how you understand about love?"

This was a clear question of representation. People applaud. Dean held the microphone on stage by girls, watching them with slime.

"Love is eternal patience." The 5th girl Yu answered at first in English, "love can be divided into two types, big Love—like God loves us, Jesus Christ died for our sins, our teachers adopt us and educate us; private love, do not have to say, everyone has. 《Bible》 said: 'Many waters cannot quench love; rivers cannot wash it away. If one were to give all the wealth of his house for love, it would be utterly scorned.'" (<<Old Testament—Song of Solomon 8:7 >>)

Applause. Dean smiled and nodded: "Very good!" He looked at other girls.

"Can I use a story to describe a kind of love?" The 2nd girl Shang then said, "Our mom said that she would like to compile a book called 《Love—The Best Gift》 She wanted to make it like a gift book, she wrote the preface for the book, said:

love, the best gift in the world;
love, the only gift in the world;
love, the reason God created all things;
love, the source of all lives;
love, the best education in the world;
love, the basic education in the world;
love, makes human been;
love, make us to close to God.

"Our mother also asked us to collect some stories about love to compile into the book. We have collected some, I'd like to tell you one of them now."

"Great, I can not wait to hear the story!" Dean encouraged her with smile, Jessie doing faithfully translated.

"There was a symphony orchestra, every player was Christian, the conductor was their pastor. Each year when Easter holiday, they went to Easter Island for concert. But this was a different year. In the morning that day, after they came to the island by ship, they heard that it would be typhoon at night on the sea. People who attended the island started to refund tickets, every one tried to catch a ship to leave the island before the typhoon arrival. However, the conductor repeated consideration, then decided to stay, he said to his orchestra: 'even if only one audience here, we would performed as usual.

"In the evening, almost everyone left the Easter Island by ships, but all members of the orchestra came to the concert hall, they were pleasantly surprised to see that there really was an audience there, the gray hair black old man was sitting in the aisle midfield side of the auditorium seat, wearing a hat. The lights were dim; no one could see his face. The orchestra performed as usual. When the playing finished, they did not hear the applause, two players could not help whispered to complain, said: 'This man did not know music, he doesn't respect our play, we came here to waste time, not as early as possible to catch the last ship to leave the hell.'

"But the conductor asked everybody continue the show until all the tracks finished playing, the applause of audience was still not on." Conductor asked the orchestra stood up, he expressed admiration and gratitude to his colleagues, then, just as every performance, he turned, facing the audience, bowed, after that, the conductor came down from stage, solemnly to the only audience, What surprised was, that he find that man had been dead.

"All players complained: 'We stayed here all night, only played for a dead man?', but they still respected their conductor, buried the old man, prayed and played a soul music for him. That night, the stormy had be rushing this island, but every body of the orchestra stayed in the Church, all were safe. Next day, the typhoon passed, all members of the orchestra came to sea shore to wait for the ship, then they heard, all people who took ship left Easter Island last night, got wreck on the sea, no one survivors.

"The conductor was looking distant at the sea, then lead every body one for the people dead. He said: 'Last night, that old man, the only one we played for, he was an angel, was God sent to save us, if not him, we might take the last ship to left last night, if in that case, we are now, not in this world any more, thank God, we live by the test. God's love saved us."

Shang' story was finished, the church broke into enthusiastic applause. The 4th girl Zhi then said that she also wanted to tell a story about love.

"There was a robust Canadian, was a climber. Once he came to Tibet, China, want to climb Mount Everest. That day on the mountain road, he saw a Tibetan girl walk in front of him, she was young and short, a little fat boy was ridding on her back, but she walked faster than the big tall Canadian. When they arrived a hillside village, Canadian took a break, he found the young girl and asked her, said:'I carry such a bag witch is not too big too heavy to climb, still feel so tired, you carried a fat boy, do not feel heavy?' Tibetan girl could not help but smiled and said: 'Sir, what you carried was a burden, what I carried was my brother.'"

Zhi won the enthusiastic applause too. The next speaker was the 1st girl Gong, she also told a story.

"There was a young man named Tony, he once borrowed a book in a library in London, he found the review in the book witch was the previous reader left, the reader's ideas and insights gave Tony deeply impressed, he found the address of the reader, then he wrote a letter to the lady named Su. Sooner, Tony was pleased to received a reply from Su, after that, they both wrote letters to each other, and talked about correspondence for all aspects of life.

"But war broke out, Tony enlisted, was sent to France to fight, he and Su had maintained communication links, in the most difficult days, Su gave Tony a great comfort and encouragement. Tony sent Su a photo of him, solemnly expressed his love, and hope Su could also send a photo to him. Su relied to Tony, said that if he really like her, he would not care about her appearance and looks, they had become ally and partner in life, and had established strong bonds of friendship. Tony felt regret, but fully agree with the views of Su.

"After two years, the war stopped. Tony returned, he wanted to immediately see Su. Su replied that they could meet at seven o'clock on Friday night, at the Bell Tower at the Central Station Square, her would hand Times Daily. Tony replied immediately agreed, saying that his hands would be holding a bouquet of roses.

"The day finally came, Tony reached Central Station early. When the bell rang at 7 o'clock, Tony then saw a blond, slim, beautiful girl came to him with smile, Tony walked to her immediately. However, the blonde girl didn't come to him, she past Tony, while behind her, a gray-haired hair, clothes worn, body fat old woman, hands holding a Times Daily, was standing under the Bell Tower looking at Tony. Tony could not believe his eyes, he even wanted to run away immediately at that moment, but then he remembered in last three years, at his most lonely, frustrating, weakest time, Su had given him a great encouragement and comfort. Tony again to restore the spirit, he straightened his uniform, holding flowers went to Su, solemn to saluted and said: 'Hello! I am Tony.' The old lady looked at Tony, smiled and said: 'Kid, I do not know how it is, but that girl just has put the paper into my hands, told me said that if a young man later holding flowers come and talk to me, please tell him to go to the

Swiss restaurant across the square, the girl will be there to wait."

With mirth and applause, the atmosphere of the church became more active. The last speaker was the 3rd girl Jiao, she also told a story:

"During the Vietnam War, a group of orphans to be temporary shelter in a refuge, the refuge hidden in the mountains, by a French doctor and two nurses to care of these children. Outside the aircraft often came to bomb. A 6-year-old girl named Ying was seriously injured, bleed a lot, she needed blood transfusions. But the blood type of doctors and nurses doesn't match hers, so the doctor asked all the children, who are willing give blood donation for Ying, if no blood transfusion, she would soon died. The doctor asked twice, a boy who was at the same age with Ying named Xiaoheng slowly raised his hand, but he immediately put down again. The doctor asked again, Xiaoheng raised his hand again. After a blood test, the doctor said that Xiaoheng can give Ying blood transfusion. The nurse helped Xiaoheng lied down in the bed by Ying, they began to do blood transfusions for them. small drops of constant blood flowed into Ying's body, the doctor took time to come visiting them, he found that Xiaoheng was silently crying, the doctor asked if Xiaoheng didn't feel discomfort, but was biting fist and shook his head. Transfusion was completed, Ying was saved. The doctor and nurses praised and thanked Xiaoheng, then asked him why he cried. Xiaoheng replied that he thought, when he gave blood to Ying, he himself would die. The doctor and nurses looked at him in amazement, then asked: 'So why did you still give blood transfusion for Ying if you thought so?' Xiaoheng said: 'Because, she is my friend.'"

Applause was heavy, but very powerful. Some ones wiped tears.

"Thank Lord!" Dean then stood on the stage, also applauded, "Well, now, Let's welcome girls' mothers and teachers—sisters Jin and Medie!"

Applause, and enthusiastically sounded. Tall and slim, wearing a blue velvet dress, Jin and Medie hold hands came to the stage, shook hands with Dean and Jessie, then they smiled and bowed to the audience. People immediately saw that they were a pair of beautiful twin sisters.

Dean said to the audience: "Before coming to Canada, Jin worked for China Philharmonic Chorus and Symphony Orchestra as a conductor, she also was a special news reporter of CCTV classical music channel. She graduated from the Central Conservatory of Music, Conducting Department, Later she was going to Germany, majored in composition and conducting, got master degree. Philharmonic Girls Chorus was founded by her. Jin's sister Medie is a life scientist, graduated from Tsinghua University, doctorate. She studied and designed digital instruments of medical testing, treatment and research, she also studied about the state of human body in deep meditation and brain in Zen, she studied Buddhist nirvana and how the relics are formed. This is a world highly sophisticated research subjection of Life Science, and she hopes to continue her research In Canada. Jin and Medie got music education by their mother in their childhood. Their family came to Canada just now, in order to make more money, Jin and Medie are doing hard labor job, they are living in government welfare apartment, looking for professional job, hope to have some information from our brothers and sisters. Ok, now, Let's enjoy more of Philharmonic girls."

Dean's successful completion of his work, exit the stage in the applause.

Applause calm down, Medie and five girls stood in a row, the audience quiet. Their sight fell on Jin's back, her slender waist upright exceptionally charming, neat light hair cascades down and around his waist. She gently lifted a hand, a song gently flying out from her hands into the air.

Audience suddenly intoxicated during, the big auditorium so quiet as if into a whole universe, only the angels singing was flying. Audiences also felt, the sounds was not sang by girls, but changed from Jin's hands, her conduction looked like a beautiful dance. An song 《Over The Rainbow》 in a cappella harmony was getting away, away, was recovered by a magician's magic. Jin's hand stopped in the air, in seven seconds of silence and recollection, Jin's hand gently put down. Audience's cheers and applause enlightening.

The audience quiet down again, the name of the tracks were showed on the big screen of both sides of the stage. Under the spot light, Medie sat by the piano, a fantastic soulful and beautiful music sounded, it's Liszt's famous 《Love Dreams》. Music came from Medie's flying fingers. After a long solo, chorus joined into. Like the moon rising from a lake, soft, clear, flowing warm love at the silent night. Medie's long hair like falls fluctuations in shiny, ups and downs with her arm and body in the music. At this moment, the piano became the main ensemble, choral became the accompaniment, the atmosphere of music was full into the hall, linger in people's ears, nourishing their hearts.

The next song, piano accompaniment by the 3rd girl Jiao, Medie and Shang sang the famous female duet 《Flowers》 which was from French composer Deli Booth's opera 《Lakmé》. Then it was two songs composed by Jin, polyphonic choral 《The Last Uncharted Of Music》 and 《Italy Quartet》. Finally, one was that song of many people were familiar 《You Raise Me Up》 —

When I am down, and, oh, my soul so weary,
When troubles come, and my heart burdened be,
Then, I am still and wait you in the silence,
Until you come and sit awhile with me.
You raise me up, so I can stand on mountains;
You raise me up to walk on stormy seas;
I am strong when I am on your shoulders;
You raise me up to more than I can be.

Many people were singing with them. Girls do have a professional level and first-class choral music skills, the audience amazed. When Dean took the stage again, the applause was still continuous.

"The wonderful scene like this, usually should appear in the end of story, but their story is just beginning. My dear friends, brothers and sisters, my sincere thanks to the Lord, made us can listen to and watch so wonderful sounds in the evening, to experience such a holy state of innocence and love created a miracle. Sincerely thank five angels and their excellent teachers. Later, you can go to the hall door to buy their CDs and DVDs, any questions about them, please ask now or later give to me. Girls will very happy to answer in order to get support from your confidence. Some body raised their hands and stood up immediately, asked loudly: "When is the next show please?"

The audience laughed, and then an enthusiastic applause. Christmas bell was ringing, the church choir took the stage, sing 《Amazing Grace》, and the last song was children chorus《Silent Night》.

Singing flied out of the church, everything of outsidc was being immersed in the songs of serene.

Snow was falling down slowly from sky, with God's message, immense.

3

COLLECTION

Jin and Medie have adopted six orphaned children, when they went to high school, they tried any way to save money, but they used money in their personal collection.

Gong collected western classical music DVDs, she wanted to become a musical architect, she studied all the world famous opera house and concert halls, she has been learning to design concert halls on computer; Shang collected classical music CDs, she has became a young violinist already; Jiao, she wanted to be a movie music composer; Zhi and Yu collected classical music information and music books, Zhi wanted to become a music columnist, and Yu wanted to be a music producer; Ark collected sheet music and Hi Fi information, he wanted to be a conductor. All the collection they put together for everybody share, made a music family.

Jin formed five girls to be a chorus, they had often been invited to participate in performances and video recordings.

In summer, after dinner, they always went a park to walk, they sing songs in the old city wall park where was near by Central Conservatory of Music, the beautiful cappella chorus attracted passers stopped to watch them. But after they came to Canada, they didn't have time to walk after dinner, they had to work hard and study hard.

When girls asked Jin why she adopted them, Jin said:

"God saw you are thirsty, he created the water, milk, juice and Coca-Cola for you; God saw you are hungry, he created bread, dumplings, pizza and McDonald's for you; God saw you are lonely, he created music, painting and dance for; God saw that you are poor and ugly no friends, he created me for you."

4

PHILHARMONIC

1

(larghetto)

Overlooking by plane from air at the shiny silvery dome of Philharmonic City main Building stands the dazzling sign—the golden harp and the huge letters PHILHARMONIC GROUP INTERNATIONAL facing three directions.

Philharmonic City, also known as Philharmonic Garden, the entire city was a major international enterprise, kept on building and developing. Philharmonic Garden was divided into six areas—B District (Business District), T District (Research and Development District), S District (Commercial Service area), E District (Education District), A District (Apartment Area) and G District (Landscaping Area).

The Philharmonic City gathers many world-renowned scientists, writers, artists, educators, scholars as well as knowledgeable people and attracts business and tourists from different countries around the world. Trees, flowers, music, fountains, sculptures, pigeons and Philharmonic ladies were everywhere and filled with world-class metropolis and the elegance of the fine Chinese civilization.

The Philharmonic City was built surrounded by mountains and rivers, with plenty of trees, skyscrapers and highway bridges looked like a modern international architectural art Fair. The streets of Philharmonic City are arranged in neat rows, connected with seven large squares, seven medium-sized plazas and seven small-sized squares. According to the number, they could be referred to them as the "The 5th Ave." or "The 11th Square. Hugo said:" Music, literature and mathematics were the three keys to open the human wisdom". Therefore, all streets of the Business were named as world-class musicians, such as Herbert von Kara Jan Ave., Schumann Street, Hayden Ave., Puccini Street, etc. The streets from apartment District were named as famous writers like Tolstoy Street, Shakespeare Street, Hemingway Ave., Kafka Ave.. The streets in University town were named as scientists such as Einstein Street, Archimedes Street, Newton Street and Galileo Street. All these street names were elected and adopted under Philharmonic City Polls. The names of Plazas in Philharmonic City were related to art and geography, such as: New World Plaza, Mexico Plaza, Greece Plaza, Pyramid Plaza, Spain Plaza, Vienna Plaza, Italy Plaza, Bohemia Plaza, etc. The architect styles of these Plazas were mixed the classic, romantic and modern.

The modern three-dimensional traffic was well-connected in Philharmonic City extending to all directions, Planet Bridges through from the 4th to the 6th stories of from philharmonic Process Design Center Building. Philharmonic City implements closed-end management and satellite monitoring system; all internal vehicles hold automatic access cards to entry and exit. There are neither police, intersection, nor traffic lights in the streets, all sections were one-way roads; everything was orderly, calm and peaceful.

Here was a world-class green standard non-smoking area, and all vehicles are without smoke and noise. It takes only 5 minutes from Philharmonic City Airport to Philharmonic City Central Square. Even travel from Jing Xi International Airport to Philharmonic City Central Station, only need to take 10 minutes by high-speed maglev train. Apartment area was built around the lake, lakeshore was covered by all kind of trees. A not very wide, long white pedestrian path lies around the lake. There was a seven-meter-wide circle green zone between the avenue and road on the hill. For every 86 meters, there will be a celebrity's statues on the grass. Public electronic advertising screens locate in the middle of the every two statues. Between the statues and electronic advertising screens, there are white benches for visitors to relax.

Philharmonic lake was even larger than the Wuhan East Lake and Hangzhou West Lake, with a total area of 8.98 square kilometers. It was the general term for Philharmonic Within Lake and Outside Lake. The Within Lake was wide and vague, with beautiful sight. It was divided into eastern and western parts. East lake part was large, close to public areas, it was called Philharmonic Lake because it was just right beside Philharmonic Island; the western Lake part was smaller, close to the tourism area, swans infest and haunt here so it's also called as

Swan Lake. Within Lake was embeds between mountains and buildings with multi-cultural styles. The perimeter of the embankment was 18 km. A two-meter-wide path and a seven-meter-wide roadside green zone area lies around the lake. In the middle of green space and the hill, there was a white long corridor surround the lake. Even when rain and snow, visitors could still enjoy the Philharmonic Lake, walk and discover the beauty of Philharmonic.

The beautiful scenery attracts many foreign and local visitors and it was the paradise on earth.

Philharmonic Lake's tributaries curved flow through the whole Philharmonic Garden. Twenty-four bridges across on the rivers. Straight White Rose Embankment connected east bank and Philharmonic Island. People could see some rare species of birds, such as egrets, white storks, herons, mandarin ducks and swans, etc. fly freely above lake. They were like elegant fairies hiding and revealing, playing, strolling, dancing in the lake or on the island to enjoy the heavenly life of freedom and tranquility. It was an ideal place for music performers to practice instructions at Philharmonic Island every morning and evening. In every morning, the first sounded on the lake was mostly an Emilia violin . . . .

2

(larghetto)

This was a silent and cold morning in winter, Philharmonic Lake was still sleeping in the darkness before dawn. There was an unkempt, untidy, around ten years old boy who's shoulders was carrying a dirty pocket, holding a rusty steel hooks, with lowed head and walking slowly along the snow-covered pedestrian path of Delta Diamond lake.

At 7 o'clock every night, the boy brought some empty bags and a flashlight came to Apartment A, try to avoid making eyes contact with people and sneaked into the garbage path of each building. He opens the exit doors of All Things Chorus the large garbage containers, drills into it and picks all kinds of recyclable waste. He sells this waste to make money. The boy always completed his work before 9PM. After that, he will sit in a corner of the garden, listen to those sound of the piano, Chinese lute, clarinet, violin, cello, trumpet, xylophone . . . . and soprano, baritone or children's vocal of practicing singing come out from windows.

The walls of apartment buildings of Philharmonic City were all made from blue glass, only the top part was in different color. Looking down from the air, an array of curved letters are arranged from south to north of lakeshore—PHILHARMONIC, the twelve letters were ordered from red-purple, purple, purple-blue, blue, blue-green, green, yellow-green, yellow, orange-yellow, orange, orange-red and red. Each letter constitutes a community. There are eight condo apartment buildings in Zone A, with green roof, the residents who live there were musicians of Philharmonic.

During each Saturday night, the boy finished his work earlier and then came to the Music School of Philharmonic University to spend two dollars, enjoy an evening music appreciation session with those students from colleges, elementary Schools or high Schools. The video was playing without light in the audiovisual classroom, no one could see him and no one knows him. When all these sounds that make him intoxicated and fascinated disappears, he will leave with anxieties and return to the small barn beside highway bridge to sleep in north of Philharmonic Garden.

The boys had been well aware of these. Six months ago, he spent one hundred twenty-eight Yuan and fifty six cents bought the waste ownership of Zone A from an boy named "Musician". In order to force him to say the reason for transfer the ownership, this tall and dark "musician" punched his body to be black and blue, but could not believe his big joke said—"I also want to be a musician".

A poor boy survived by collecting and selling scrap, but dare to say that he wanted to be a musician! Was he making a day dream! It was really ridiculous!

"How much is a musician worth? I am gonna transferred the nickname to you, alright?"

The boy was lying on the ground, nose was bleeding, shook his head.

After that day, the skinny tinny boy had been struggling in hunger and illness, almost died. His worn hut was filled with bottles, waste and lot of used books, he fall asleep tiredly in disappointment and hope. His daily tears from the heart only mean a dream—mother and music.

Now the winter was here, the air was so cold. It was an ordinary morning for the lonely poor boy. A long of footprint was on the path which was covered by heavy snow beside the dark blue lake in the morning. This footprint past by those public advertisement screens and the musician statues—Bach, Wagner, Verdi, Vivaldi, Mozart, Beethoven, Schubert, Haydn, Debussy, Rossini, Puccini, Schumann, Chopin Liszt, Berlioz, Grieg, Dvorak, Brahms, Sibelius, Strauss, Mendelssohn, Mahler, Smetana Tana, Bizet, Saint-Saens, Bartok, Schoenberg, Elgar,

Rachmaninoff, Shostakovich . . . . long way left immortal impression in his mind, but he knew that this was just the beginning of his life, he found a starting point for himself, his minds wandering in this starting point all days, he hopes someone can really take him on the road. As usual, he finally came to the front of the statue of Tchaikovsky.

The boy loved Tchaikovsky, because he had listened to Tchaikovsky's 《Swan Lake》. "The melody of the music was forever graved in the dream of the boy. In his mind, Tchaikovsky was like a grandfather, and he seemed never to be young before, the boy could not imagine a young Tchaikovsky. Standing before the statue, the boy looked up Tchaikovsky's full of sad faces. The boy's heart raised up a bit of sadness. The sadness was so deep, he thought that it was Tchaikovsky's spirit attached in his body. The boy sadly overlooked those small islands in Swan Lake with Tchaikovsky. At this moment, the boy would always thought of his parents and those good times before at school. But he lost, all of them, in one day, in the earthquakes. The fate brought him to be here, with solitude and wandering hopes; he has been looking for his own, looking for his idol, and looking for his most beautiful Swan Lake witch was in his heart. Where he would rebirth his new life and soul. At the front of marble base of the statue, engraved in Chinese, British and Russian:

1840_1893
Russian musicians
Peter Ilyich Tchaikovsky

"Tchaikovsky" sat in the chair, looked down at the boy, and the boy always want to sit on the chair by Tchaikovsky. From this position to look at Swan Lake and

Philharmonic Island, the view was the most beautiful. The boy dropped his back and hook on the ground, trembling rubbed his frozen ears and said: “It’s so cold today, sir.” He talked with Tchaikovsky but didn’t want to look at him, if so, wind would drill in his neck. He leaned on the base of Tchaikovsky sculpture, sat down on his broken bag, put his frozen hands in sleeves, then started to wait.

The lake was still dark, quiet and a little bit windy. The long White Rose Embankment and Philharmonic Island were still in the dreams. If it was in the summer, those electronic advertising screens would be already shut down at this time. The boy looked at the electronic advertising screen witch was on his left, there was a photo of Tchaikovsky and his words:

> “Music is the greatest gift to mankind from God—the gift for Rangers in darkness.”

The light of the screen reflected on the snow, the boy curled his body in the black coat, leaned against the statue, closed his eyes wearily. He could sit down on the bench to have a rest, but that would too cold, he would fall asleep immediately, and he maybe freezing to death.

It had been six months, every early morning, the boy came to this place on time, sat there, lifted up his childish face in front of Tchaikovsky statue, and looked at the Philharmonic Island. Every time at this moment, his eyes become much bright, full of piety and vitality, waited here alone silently. He could hear the sound of wind and water, trees shook off raindrop, the mist floating, even the sound of souls of those statues’ and the sound of birds witch fog disturb their dreams, and also the sound of heartbeat of this frozen silent boy's pray for dawn in the chilly early morning.

After these prelude, finally, a gentle, graceful and slightly sad violin music came from the willows shadow of Philharmonic Island, it flew by the edge of the boy's dream, flew to the sky, flew to the lake, mountains. The music seemed want to comfort those statue's souls, soft, gentle and beautiful. The sound of music was pure, clear, and bright, the echo flew on the lake and in the air and touched everything with a angel's hand. The boy was smiling, tears silently running down from his cheeks.

The boy always reached this place at 5:30 in the morning and listened to the violin played by an unknown player who he had never met and even could not see the shadow from the Philharmonic Island. The boy sat there, enjoyed the sad but powerful music that lift him out from darkness, cold, hunger, the music brought him warm, hope and brightness and strengths. No matter sunny or raining, snowing or windy, the magnificent music shone his heart and body, like sunrise every morning. During this six months, the player of the violin occasionally didn't come out, maybe got sick, whenever, the boy would still sat there for forty minutes, kept a fixed posture, motionless, as if an invisible violin being played for him, and only played for his. Forty minutes later, the boy would still sit there for a little while, trying to retain precious memory of that dream, didn't want to leave. Finally, he leaned on the statue, stood up, pick up his bag and hook, said bye to Tchaikovsky, then walked away along the lakeshore. He walked past those statues quietly, he has been so familiar with these faces of each statue, that he was able to memorize the names of each players, composers and conductors, their nationality and date of birth and death.

The boy honored, loved them blindly, and the only reason of all of these, just because of the song witch was played by that violin every morning. He believed that the music beautiful like that must come from heaven, and these musicians must be also the angels of heaven, so that his daily happiness came from the 40 minutes to be brought into heaven.

Walking along the lakeshore, the boy had imagined the composer and player of the violin song for hundred times, he looked at each statue and try to find out the notes, the temperament, brilliance and the inspiration of that music. He wanted to see the player on the island, but in the early morning, the Philharmonic Island was not open to public, only for musicians. One month ago, the boy had heard a violin song from a car witch was parked at New World Plaza, he found out that was right the sound of that violin witch he was so familiar.

"Yes, it must be him!" The boy was so excited and he stood beside the blue car until the music was finished. A foreign little girl in the car had been staring at him. But the boy still didn't know the name of the player. He hoped one day that he could see the player and his violin. But he had to be like this only, stood at lakeshore when no body was here, in myriad of hopes before dawn, looked forward the first light of morning. Philharmonic Island became a island of his hope, the island of his home, the island of his mother and it entrusts with his unlimited desire and worship. The violin sound became his reverie, his soul and faith. The distance from him to the island was perhaps equals the distance between music and him. When could he be end of the ugly duck ranger life, to become a White Swan, opened his wings flying to his dreaming place. Music, how come music had such magic power to make a homeless, cold, hungry and poor kid to dream so much?!

The boy came in every morning to front of the statue of Tchaikovsky like crazy, disregarding the weather to listen to the song from heaven which is instrumented by the unknown player. This is the happiest time in his days, and his heart was like a swan flying freely with the melody . . . .

3

(Allegro moderato)

As an usual day, the boy was in hunger, sleepiness and cold came here with the heart full of hope and dedication. Before today, he had not been hearing the sound of the violin for ten days.

Philharmonic Island was still quiet, nothing happened. Where was his friend? What was he doing? was he coming today? Did he worry about his playing would be too hard in such cold and dark morning? Did he know that there was a loyal fan looking forward to hear his music every morning at the other side of the lake? Yes, he must be able to see and feel it, because music was the best bridges of communication between hearts. When the boy thought of this, his hands were not cold but more flexible and strong; his heart also became warm and bright. He was waiting.

It was still so quiet around. At 5:30, the boy sat there firmly. When the wind bursts snowflakes, gently slides into the lake, under the shallow of willows from the Philharmonic Island, where the angel was but nobody can see, the sound of the violin started again!

It quietly gracefully flew to the whole Philharmonic Island, the Swan Lake, a new day finally started. How excited the boy was, liked to see his family after a long absence, when he heard the first note, he stood up, looking at the Philharmonic Island and tears dropped from his eyes.

How wonderful it was, the first day of the New Year, he purposes that the violin wouldn't be played again, but it was actual played, played for him only, it was played for him to greet the new day, the new year, the new hope, This was his dawn. The boy put his entire body and mind into the music, he nestled in the warm embrace of the music, smiling and crying liked nobody around. He was impressed by the music deeply. A humankind boy, whose soul was flying to heaven. He stood there, at the lakeshore of his dream, but his soul was already soaring. He looked at Philharmonic Island, stood in front of Tchaikovsky statue, he looked like a tiny statue. This tiny statue belonged to the music, just like the other ones behind him.

The music was playing, the boy stood at the lakeshore, the music was showering his whole body and his heart, recharging him, giving him strength. In human's mind, there were a lots places belong to the darkness. But this boy at this moment was whole body bright, because he was undergoing re-born; His soul was birthing and burning by music. He was full inspired and shined so thoroughly, sacred. All angels were surround of him, the music was hugging him, his wings were growing out, and all thing at this moment had been remitted into eternity. Suddenly, the boy's hands raised up, he started to conduct the music by his familiar melody. Everything became a huge orchestra, wind flew over head, trees shook, everything started flying upward. The thin boy was raising up his head, flame was erupting from his soul through his waving arms, the boy at this moment became to be the center of lightness and the conductor of all things chorus.

4

(Allegretto)

40 minutes, it finally end. The boy put down his arm slowly, his eyes still looked straight ahead, his face turned All Things Chorus red shiny, his breath was powerful. He did not turned back and leave the lakeshore as usual, but still stood straightly there, feel the sound of the violin was still flying on the lake. He tries to retain it, the remarkable brilliant moment, until cold wind blew his body so that he could not help trembling.

At the moment of dawn, the fog had not dispersed. The boy gradually calmed down. He suddenly felt so tired, he was like a child missing his mother's embrace, and he really wanted to keep standing there, to pursue his dream, became a statue. But, when it was 6 o'clock, the security car past here, they will take him away immediately. The boy had to move his sour legs, he rubbed wet eyes, cheered up and picked up his bag. When was he ready to leave, the boy looked at Tchaikovsky to say goodbye to his old friend. But suddenly, he saw something on the chair of the statue by Tchaikovsky.

"What's that?" the boy took a closer look and saw a plastic bag. The boy curiously took the bag from Tchaikovsky's foot, then, he saw a book with golden cover in the bag.

The name of the book was<<The Biography Of Tchaikovsky>>, then, the boy saw a red color envelope in the book with a sentence on the envelope:

"To the boy who listened to the music every morning with Tchaikovsky"

The boy was so surprised, he could not believe his eyes, and he felt that he was in a dream. The read the words on the envelope many times, his heart beat so fast and his face turned red. The boy sat down in front of Tchaikovsky again, his heart almost jumped out of chest. He opened the envelope with the his tremble hands, he took out the paper, and saw a purple concert ticket and two hundred Yuan.

"It's new year today," the boy said to Tchaikovsky, "a miracle will happen." He carefully opened the papers, he smiled rose fragrance. With the words he could understand, the boy started reading the letter slowly:

My dear friend:

Happy New Year!

Although we never met each other, but have been very familiar____ I want to say that you are my most loyal friend, listeners, and bosom friend. I decided to use a special way to express my respects, gratitude and blessing upon you.

I know it was occurred mudslides last year in your hometown Sichuan, you have lost parents, home and school, you came to Beijing from Sichuan alone, to look for your relatives, but could not find. You had to make a living by picking up waste to sell, people call you "Garbage Boy". I know you have saved almost all the used books and paper, you have primary and secondary school textbooks for each grade level, you have many dictionaries. You have been in extremely difficult conditions, a hostile environment, constantly learning. I know you were the best student at school, you also are a faithful reader of 《Philharmonic Daily and love classical music, you have a sensitive and intelligent and strong heart. This is your precious talent God-given to you. I know why you came to Philharmonic, because here is the cradle of hope where you have been longing for. But you do not have any proof and guarantees, and you didn't meet any body to help you, so you could not go to the Hope Primary School. I know why you would come A_A apartment; I know every time when you pass by Bohemia Plaza, you would put some coin in the case of that blind flute player (in fact he was not for making money); you saw a little girl was sitting at the roadside crying, you just took her to find her mother, and bought ice cream for her. What a kind of you are, but how come there was no one to help you? I think perhaps this is God left you to my fate. I am sure you are a good seed and you will grow up.

Every morning, you came here, listened to my violin, it was probably for half a year. I saw from beginning, but I took too long to know you. You sat there so quiet, from far away, looked like a part of that sculptor. But I am thinking about your heart? What world looks like? One day, I finally came to where you live.

It was a cold, rain and snow night, I saw you in the apartment downstairs, I decided to secretly follow you, I went to Philharmonic Park, the bridge north of the gospel. I didn't know that where you live was so far, so simple, the road was so bad to go in a very dark place, and I almost slipped a few times. You live in a hut under the bridge, lit the dim light reading, I remembered you were reading a paragraph:

"I found the music world, I have been unhappy, I was short and thin, often ill, pale, often not happy, and bronchitis and the like plagued by disease and then to the old, have a piano, suddenly I found my world, I felt in a strong, I began to flourish, grow very high; I began to engage in physical exercise, access to all kinds of medals, which all are simultaneously my life completely changed. The only explanation, and the secret was: I found my sky, where I felt very safe. This was music. I was under the wings to protect her, which I have in their homes, then no one can hurt me, make me feel pain."

After reading this, then you cried. I know that, although it was the musical experience of master Bernstein's but also your heart, your soul is kind of a living person. In this moment I've got known you, and decided to do my best to help you. You have what others have, and you also have what a lot of people do not have, you also have what many people discarded. So I'd like to say that you are rich, all your wealth is your mind with a pursuit of light, the pursuit of beauty and noble, full of hope and love, and extraordinary heart.

Now let me tell you ____ every morning, that song you heard from me playing, it was "D Major Violin Concerto" composed in 1878 by Peter Ilyich Tchaikovsky the great nineteenth-century Russian musician. Since this concerto was born, had touched countless hearts in the world. But it's very difficult to play, has been the master track to be selected to measure a violinist's touchstone. The first time I heard of it was in Beijing the Great Hall Of People with my mother when I was 7 years old. The world-famous conductor Zubin Mehta, Israel Philharmonic Orchestra's and the top violinist Isaac Perlman. Perlman uses a Stradivari violin with three hundred years of history.

Perlman is a disabled musician, had polio since childhood, when he walked on stage on crutches, the (Meta Masters behind him, he took it for the piano), the audience immediately on the outbreak applause, many people are tempted to his seat and stood up to the extraordinary performer that high esteem. Perlman bow to enthusiastic Chinese audience, frequently pay tribute. Performance process, people within City Hall were silent, only musician's sound in virtually ruffles the emotional waves of people. As the venue was too large to use loudspeakers, so the sound was not ideal. Perlman sat in a chair, with his whole body and mind to express, the most brilliant movement of Tchaikovsky's art life. His superb acting, broad and deep human emotion of love and passion, this first classic on its head, with the sound of the piano to conquer all the audience. The playing was so wonderful, master Perlman sweated a lot, until the end of the song completely. Audience for the musicians superb performance to hold a long applause. Master tried to stand up to answer the curtain call, but he was too tired, he played for long time, he tried three times but failed. The violinist came to help him, but declined, he stubbornly insisted to be up by himself. Palmer tried once again, then dropped into the chair again. The audience could no longer suppress their feelings, all stood up to applaud for the extraordinary artist. At the 6th time, he finally succeeded. He stood up, looked up, suddenly opened his arms to his sincere admiration and loving Chinese audience, gave them a happiest smile, then bowed deeply. Many audience's tears running, for the success of the musician' spirit and his artistic, for his noble character, outstanding talent and a deep admiration and endless praise.

I will never forget that concert, Isaac. Perlman, so I got know a lot more meaningful than the music itself. So far, it was still my deepest feelings of a concert, I think that is the greatest concerto.

Six months ago, my right arm had surgery, in order to recover as soon as possible, I insist on practicing every day. During this time, I almost did not attend a concert. But you have virtually gave me great encouragement, I am touched by you. I would like to say thanks to you.

It's the day of new year today, Philharmonic Concert Hall will hold a New Year's Concert tonight, Philharmonic International Symphony Orchestra will play the greatest works of Tchaikovsky. Now, I officially invite you to come with me and my mother tonight to the concert, you can watch me to play this Violin Concerto, just like every morning you listen to it. And the conductor tonight is my mother Jin Qin. You should believe in yourself and are fully qualified to enjoy this beautiful and sublime moments. I would be very happy if you would come to my first premiere. Please sit in the front row, I will have more courage and confidence when I se you there.

In addition, if you want to, you can live with my family. My mother has adopted me and other four girls. I told her every thing about you. After a full investigation and understanding, we have your situation, proof of home, all written reports submitted Philharmonic Hope Primary School, they have agreed to receive you if my mother can guarantee for you. You will have a new home, new family, you can re-access to formal learning opportunities, to receive the best education in schools. Your dreams are the most legitimate rights of a child, and now, this community right back to you again, cherish it, your future is secure. The city Philharmonic is your home, your choice was right, your hope and trust in her finally got return, I am really happy for you!

Please wait for me and my mother at 5pm at the door of the concert hall. I know, it's not the first time to you coming to the concert hall, but tonight, you do not have to watch the show in hungry, we will have dinner with you together. I hope that you can be punctual for appointments.

At last, I wish you have a happy great birthday! Today, you are ten years old, but I know, your heart is over this age. I hope that all wonderful music will accompany you in your whole life, give you eternal happiness and bright!

Sincerely Yours,
Shang (I'm a 14 years old girl)

Garbage boy had read the letter, afford to sit there. Two lines of melted snow water was flowing down from Tchaikovsky's cheeks.

This morning, the first car on the road passing through here, the man in the car was surprised to see a bedraggled boy sitting in the lake, head leaning against the statue next to Tchaikovsky, no one else to tears, his chest tightly holding a golden book.

> Music is the greatest gift from God to mankind—a gift to the homeless in the darkness.
>
> —Tchaikovsky

5

After 15 years, the boy became a music architect and a choral conductor. Some one says that this boy was a reincarnation of a music master; some one say: in the fact, each of us, everything in the world, all are the embodiment of music.

5

Return Freedom Back To Birdcage

In 1999 Summer, Jin had interview the Sixth International Children's Choir Festival in the Forbidden City Concert Hall of Beijing. From Russia, the United States, Finland, Denmark, Japan, Hong Kong, Mexico, a total of twelve countries and regions, fifteen children choirs, dressed in colorful national costumes, like the groups of happy birds, they stage an exhibition crisp, bright voice. No body does not envy them, where people will see the smiles like flower on their faces, hear the angelic singing and moving, felt the peace, love and harmony. Jin felt like being in paradise, all boys and girls look sweet and innocent infected everyone.

Intermission, Jin sat between Canadian choir and American, she wanted to talk to these children to share their festival, Jin would also like to know that they came to Beijing during the summer vacation, spend a lot of rehearsal time, whether it would affect their study? Did they have a lot of home work like Chinese students? Did they have to learn computer, arts, music even more just like many Chinese children . . . .

"Hello, my name is Jin Qin, and I'm a special correspondent of CCTV music channel. May I have your name please?"

Jin started her questions to the 12 year-old American boy.

"Hi, my name is Andy Lake. Nice to know you! Mrs. Qin."

"Nice to meet you too! Andy." Jin shook hands with him, "Is this your first time to China?"

"Yes it is."

"What grade are you in at school? Andy."

"I am going to be grade 7."

Then Jin asked him about his home work in summer vacation, their talking has attracted several children who next to them.

Andy said that they could take six months to do the home work of summer vacation. Jin was more curious and asked him what was their home work.

Andy said: "Our teacher asked us to choose 26 countries, the first letter of the name of each country can not be same, according to alphabetical order, such as A, I chose Australia (Australia), B I chose Britain (UK), C I chose China . . . . we have to collect many information about these 26 countries, compiled into a book, including administrative map, flag, topography, climate, population, history, science, culture, property, resources, art, education, etc., to be illustrated to do."

"So complicated!" Jin praised.

"No, this is very interesting!" Andy smiled, "I've got a lot of information! I also collect stamps from 26 countries, many images. I also have collected the national music of these countries and their national map with their characters."

"Wow! You must be very great! Andy. How did you get that?" Jin can not hide her admiration.

"On internet, I found out the website of their Ministry of Education, their post office or some other web site, then I E-mail them, tell them that I am an American school student, and I am compiling a book, I want their national maps, stamps and a few of the most famous folk music. They really replied, sent me many information! I'm going to make all of these multimedia pages on my blog and make CD, each country is accompanied by their characters and pictures with their music as the background music. Yesterday, I also got an e-book <<Complete of Chinese Culture>>. "

Andy looked very proud. Jin could see it from his face and envy of this open education to bring these children lots of fun from creative. As what the Chinese ancients said: Interesting is better than learning, enjoy is better than interesting.

"Then Andy what was your winter vacation home work?" Jin asked.

"That was a writing, <<The History of something>>. According to your interesting, free topics, such as I wrote <<The History of Baseball>>, I am a baseball fan."

"This topic is not small!" Jin sighed.

"We wrote this subject, too." a Canadian girl who sat behind them said, "I wrote <<The History Of Children Chorus>>. Some of my classmates wrote<<The History Of Space Development Of Human>>, <<The History Of Calculators>, <<The History Of North American Immigration>>. Also somebody wrote such as <<The Owners Of Violin Stradivarius>>, <<The History Of

Human Destruction of the ecological environment>>. My sister Eleanor wrote<<The Thinnest History>>, she criticized how harsh the school bell in many countries is, and had been never changed in hundred years."

"That's true!" Another white boy said, "My brother Jeff wrote<<The History Of School > >, he hopes that in future, every body can choose his favorite school, teachers and courses on internet on the global."

"That's great!" Every body agreed.

"So what did you write about?" Jin asked him.

The white boy smiled, said: "What I wrote was<<The History Of mine>>I predicted that I would be a great software developer in future, these new software would change human's life a lot, and my whole life would spent in this way!"

"Ha ha ha ha!" Many people laughed, everybody looked happy.

That day, when was the end of the performances, Jin asked a high school girl of Chinese choir. "How much home work for your Summer vacation?"

"Tons of them! My mother even also asks me do more, sick of it!" She pushed the glasses up and shakes head. Got home, Jin asked the 5th girl Yu that if the teacher asked her to write an article about what the history of, what would she write. Yu felt interest in it immediately, she thought a moment, her sisters were watching TV, Yu saw a bird was jumbling in a small cage, then she answered: "Mom I want to write <<The history of birds>>."

At that night, Jin could not sleep, she thought of a poet's words: "Open the cage, let the bird fly away, return freedom back to the cage." To all children with heavy wings, when can we return happiness back to their childhood?

6

ENCOURAGEMENT

In summer vacation, Jin took Ark and five girls to watch International Acrobatics Festival performances, Ark particularly fond of the clown, clown always amused the audience laugh.

Back to school, teacher asked students to write a composition about what they want to do when they grow up. Students wanted to be managers, doctors, lawyers, scientists, engineers, writers, police officers or teachers, but the girl Zhi said that she wanted to be a clown.

Her teacher were very surprise: "There are so many job can do, but how come you only want to be the worst one?!"

Zhi felt very unfairly treated.

Later, Zhi emigrated to Canada with family. At the new school, she got a same composition question; Zhi still wrote that she wanted to be a clown.

Teacher's comment was: "I hope you can play like the comic master Chaplin, bring happiness to everybody in the world!"

In the fact, Zhi was not really want to be a clown, she wanted to be a music columnist, but she enjoyed the clown's show, and t the teacher's encouragement made her feel so happy.

In the first year to be Canada, Jin took more than 40 minutes every day to go to work by bicycle, she had to cross a high bridge to over highway 401, that was a long bridge, she did not have enough strength to ride up to the bridge, but always pushed her bicycle to cross it. She was tired, she was doing a hard labor job. One day, when she pushed the bicycle onto the bridge, she saw a black old man riding came to her, when he was passing by Jin, Jin heard him say:

"Hi! Come on! You're young and strong!"

Jin did not even see his face, but she knew the one she met was an angel.

After that day, Jin was no longer pushing bicycle onto the bridge, but ride every time. An invisible force made her feel really become young and strong. And since, in many difficulties and pressures, the sound will be sounded in her ear, then she will bravely overcome his own cowardice and weakness, to meet the challenge.

When you took a dream, first time came to a strange place, what do you most need?

Jin's colleague Edith often encouraged her, said: "Good job!", "Excellence!"

Although Jin was only a temporary employee in the big company with thousand people, due to lack of experience, and sometimes made some small mistakes, but her manager William showed her smile every day, paid patience to help her solve problems. William was very good at encouraging his employees, so every body liked him, respected him. When some employees praised his good job, William would sincerely answered: "Thank you to encourage me!"

Youth cellist Pablo. Casals had been longing for Vienna, but he said: he dare not come into the city by one step, for him, the souls of Haydn, Mozart and Beethoven and other masters were still here. The first time on the stage in the Philharmonic Hall, due to tension, his bow actually flew out of Casals' hand, flew over the audience's head of first row. But Vienna's audience has shown exceptional qualities of music, silence, someone picked up the bow, one by one carefully pass over, to re-transfer back the hands of Casals. At this time, Casals was feeling, he has truly become a member of Vienna.

This was the most meaningful lesson Jin has learned since she came to the new country. She hoped that everyone had been received such an understanding, encouragement, respect and tolerance, also would give others the same love.

Any music would have its audience. At night, Jin often alone to listen to Casals played Bach unaccompanied cello divertimento. An old man was sitting in a cold, damp church under the skylight, with a musical interpretation of life. It was a dialogue between man and God, which contains the beauty and divinity of human love as deeply imbued with the moon in Jin's heart.

7

SILENT FLUTE

When the birthday of the 3rd girl Jiao 7-year-old, she received unexpected gift—a flute—was from Fat Duck a same age boy of their neighbor, Fat boy's parents forced him to learn flute, but he hated it. Fat boy's mother angrily then just gave the flute to Jiao.

But Jin felt difficult, because she adopted five children, she could not afford flute teacher for Jiao.

A few weeks later, Jin came back from work, she heard Jiao was playing a scale with a flute etude, very nice.

"Who taught you? Jiao!" Jin was surprised and asked.

Jiao smiled and said: "Fat boy's mother gave me free."

After six months, fat boy gave up piano again, but Jiao played flute very well already. One day, because of a little thing, Fat boy fought with Jiao, then made a excuse to recaptured the flute from Jiao.

Jiao cried all night, because she knew, although they had a piano at home, mother taught them five sisters every day, but Jin would no more money to buy another flute for Jiao.

However, Jiao used wood stick, rolling paper to made of a silence flute, looking for her dreams. Sometimes, people heard Jiao sang some wonderful songs, then the neighbors saw five girls showed on TV, they had been the members of National Symphony Orchestra women and children Chorus, and they would abroad to perform.

Later, someone asked Jiao: "Why did not you play the flute any more?"

Jiao said: "I myself am just a flute."

Music is in our hearts, and does not have to look outside for a instrument. This was the revelation that Jiao gave to us.

Jin bought Jiao a new flute when her 8 years old birthday.

Many years later, in the other side of the Earth, in the city Toronto, at a night in summer, Jiao was standing on the balcony of their apartment building to play flute, "Free Flight", so bright and melodious and all the stars intoxicated.

Jin asked Jiao: "How do you understand about music?"

Jiao looked at the stars sky, said: "The universe is a giant, when the first time it heard a humming song by its own sings, it was very happy and its eyes shined the light of wisdom. The blue planet we are living on is the most brightest beam of light in the eyes of the universe giant."

The Legendary Of Artists

It was raining outside, the sky was already getting dark, Gong walked into a French Art shop where was at the corner of Bloor and Yonge Street, next to the coffee shop.

She moved slowly to enjoy each painting in the shop, as if she was not the last half hour of today's final customers, and did not mind the rain wet her hair, and the staff Nick was preparing to close the shop door. Nick was busy with packing, while looked at this young Asian lady, her focus calmly looked like the Louver in the appreciation of the works. The last ten minutes to close the door, Nick still did not disturbed Gong.

Gong' s footsteps stopped in front of a painting witch was hanging on the center of the Western wall, the former location of the photograph, her face was showing a amazement, as if was struggling to identify and remember something, Nick stood behind her, she did not aware.

The painting showed a rainy day, the place was in China on a sculpture gallery of antique street, a stone road to suffer an antique calligraphy and painting shops and craft shops, some Chinese and foreign tourists were reluctant meantime, beside the street, sale some cheap jewelry, folk art and flavor of food small traders. Prominently on the picture was a two-story red antique building, named "Rong Bao Zhai." At the door of Rong Bao Zhai beside the street, a girl wore a white dress was sitting there concentrating on painting, rain soaked all the features, including a gray-haired old lady behind the girl, she was holding a red umbrella above the painting girl's head.

The painting had not price label, the sign was at the lower right corner to see the time was 5 years ago, the name of painting was <<Artists>>, and on the label said: "The painting is the collection of the store."

"May I ask who the artist of this painting is?" Gong turned to Nick,. "Can I meet him please?"

Nick did not say anything but took out his cell phone to dial. Soon he turned to Gong said:

"I'm sorry! Lady, our boss is now in Italy, could you be back after two weeks?"

Two weeks later, the same evening, the same rainy day.

"Excuse me, miss, our boss is in French, also going to Amsterdam next week to attend the auction, I am afraid, you have to wait two more weeks."

It took another two weeks, the day got dark early. Gong hold a picture to get in the French art shop, she carefully placed the picture on the counter, asked Nick help to open the package. Nick peeled the wet plastic poly film and the wrapping paper inside, at last, he saw a painting witch was almost same like that one <<Artist>> on the wall.

"I paint it by the memory." Gong pointed to the girl on the painting, said, "This is me, I gave my painting a name, called <<The Legendary Of Artists>>. Please ask your boss, I want to know who was the old lady on the painting, I want to see her today in the Thanksgiving day, I'd like to express my gratitude for 5 years ago."

It was still raining outside. Gong stood out of the art shop beside the street, looking attentively at lights of Yonge Street, listening to the bell sound of the streetcars, she smiled coffee in the humid air. 5 years ago, she was a junior high school student, she lived in City Philharmonic where was a satellite city west of Beijing. On weekend, Gong often went to Philharmonic antique culture street to paint. However, she didn't know when she was a young girl in very poor painting techniques, there was an old foreign lady who was from the other side of the glob, on a rain day, had ever hold a red umbrella for Gong, in order to enable her to concentrate on painting instead to be the rain interrupted. At that time, Gong was doing exercises, completely unaware of an angel behind her to help. This angel unknowingly come, but also in unconsciously left. Until 5 years later, fate took Gong to be this side of the glob, in her short life, she saw numerous paintings of the famous great masters in books and on internet, but only this time, she really saw a spirit higher than artistic, it did not come from the work itself, but from the artist's soul.

"Ms. Lynn had been to China in 5 years ago, <<Artists>> was she painted by the photo of her friend took for her at that time." Nick said, "Ms. Lynn is very cherished the painting, the same as a artist, she said this is the one of her favorite painting."

An umbrella was propped up above Gong's head, this time she felt, she turned around, she saw, they were familiar from the beginning, a young Eastern artist, an elderly Western artist, shook hands, then hugged tightly. Nick took a picture for them at this precious moment.

"Mrs. Lynn," said Gong with tears, "Until today, I really completed that painting of my 5 years ago."

"Yes, darling," Eighty-year-old Mrs. Lynn smiled, "Yes, you have grown up, you done yourself."

"Thanks God, 5 years ago sent me an angel!" said Gong.

"Thanks God, after 5 years, also sent me an angel!"

9

Sunrise

After a long boring midnight, the aircraft will arrive in Rome. The early light of the dawn through the porthole, has gradually diffuse into the quiet cabin. Jo was calmly looking out the window, the deep blue sky on the horizon, clouds was rapidly rolled, light rays through the cloud mantle sky, the clouds gradually dyed orange-red, red Shining burning desire. Medie sat by Jo, when she woke up and immediately attracted by scene, just liked Jo, her eyes stared without blink at out of the window.

Red spread rendering, Medie saw God's palette was changing magically in its the invisible giant pen. Horizon liked a curtain being pulled to open a corner, the sun just liked the world protagonist at its first time to show on the stage, when all life seemed to be creeping bent over its feet, and silently call for and await the arrival of its visit.

Solemn, mysterious and great, the God of Sun was rising slowly in quiet and dignified, it exposed a golden forehead, face, chest, body; Thus, Jo's forehead, face, chest and body, also reflected an instant into gold.

The new sun was shining tremblingly, suddenly leaped out of clouds and changed to be a totally independent, radiant, huge round ball, it was so fresh, bright red, such as washing. Its unparalleled beauty, it was the God of Gods. It was endowed with the beauty of all things, all things jubilant also praised its glorious life. A new world was born, a new sun also raised in Jo's heart. The sun saw this new world, the world finally saw the new sun. It saw Jo, Jo was praising it from heart with a brilliant symphonic poem, said: "Hello! My sun."

The darkness receded under the fuselage like ebb, the cabin had all been illuminated. Jo's eyes still were staring at the bright sun without blink, at this moment, his face looked like the sun god's son was generally brilliant. Medie felt so surprised to see all of this, she was shocked by this face. Yes, Medie had never seen such a sacred and pious face, from this face and the eyes, she felt that the sun was rising from Jo's heart, as if after a very long night was finally born out, and before that, Jo has been waiting for it in his heart, it seemed that his earlier life were waiting for the calm and unique Sunrise. Medie was intoxicated at this time that Jo was full of heroic qualities and looked impressed. Medie smiled and said gently:

"You must change from a bird, sir."

From last night after the first time Medie saw Jo on the plane, this man had been in a semi-comatose state of meditation, but now, he seemed was born. Jo smiled and asked:

"What does that mean? Madam."

At the same time, he still faced the glare of the sun, didn't look at the beautiful lady. Medie has been waiting for him to wink, but he didn't.

Jo's face was full of fear and an extraordinary inner strength, Medie started to worship him:

"In addition to birds, sir, only Giordano Bruno would like to look at the sun directly same like you."

"Giordano Bruno." Jo repeated one, smiled, still staring at the sun.

"Yes, he was a pioneer of human light." Medie looked out the window, said, "because the spread heliocentric, view them as rebellious church, he was burned the on the Flowers Plaza in Rome. That morning, Bruno was tied on high Cross, he was the first one to see the sunrise, he looked at sun without wink, until death. And those people below him gathered at the plaza, soldiers, clergy and executioner, all submerged in the dark, there were no least bit bright in their heart. That year, the human walked into the seventeenth century."

"Melt in the sunshine, Bruno, was not he?" Jo said, seemed to talk to the sun.

"Yes, sir, he was originally one with the sun, he was born for it, he was took away by sun. Bruno was the son of the sun."

"Are you a poet? lady." Jo smiled when he finally recovered eyes.

"No, I'm not." Medie replied. Then, she suddenly shocked, because until now she discovered, Jo was a blind man!

"The sunrise today is not same with the past." Jo said with a smile "Oh, actually," Medie said, "Actually, it's my first time to watch the sunrise on airplan."

"Oh." Jo smiled, "but for somebody, once is enough. It's great, isn't it?"

"Yes, it is. Can you . . . . can you see the sun? sir." Medie looked at the sun outside the cabin, then looked at Jo, carefully inquire.

"Yes I can, it is in my heart." Jo replied, "I like the sunrise, or I feel like the sunrise, I always imagine it, all of memory are from 30 years ago, the impression of a sunrise. When I was a child, I heard my grandfather said that the eyes of birds can look directly at the sun, the birds ranged between human and God. I wanted to change myself to be a bird, not only can fly, also can look directly at the sun, can be close to God. So I tried to do that in a morning when I took airplane with my grandpa flying over Rome like a bird, like today, I looked directly at the sun for a long time, of course I did not become a bird, I did not see God in fact, since that, I could see nothing any more. I don't know whether that was the last time I see sunrise, I hope not."

"I don't hope so either, sir." Medie felt so sad for Jo.

"Thank you."

"So, could you tell me, what do you do? sir." Medie asked, she want Jo relax a bit.

"I, music composer ____ you? Medie?" Jo smiled.

At the middle night boarding, sat down by Jo, Medie had made a phone call, Jo heard of Medie' sister called her name on the phone, his musician's ears were wonderful, but Medie thought that he had been sleeping.

"I study life sciences, sir." Medie answered.

Jo smiled: "Great. So do you like music? Medie." Jo asked slowly.

"Oh, I do, sir. Every body loves music, just like we love sun."

Jo nodded. Then he put his hand on the scores book and said: "This is a manuscript of an opera, I took almost three years to write it, finally completed now, it will be showed in the evening on February 17 at Flowers Square in Rome, I will conduct the concert, I hope you and your family come to listen."

Medie saw the title on the sheep music: <<Son of the Sun—dedicated to Giordano Bruno 400th anniversary of his death>>."

"Oh! My goodness! This is really great!" She said excitedly.

"This is a sunrise after long dark night." Jo said.

Medie hold Jo's hand, they were no more talking. Aircraft flew like a bird to over the sky of Rome right now, they looked out of the window at the newborn sun. It was the first dawn of the new year.

10

BALLET ON THE BALANCE BEAM

The wind was so strong that night, almost around midnight, Suraj Ram Closed the piano score, turned off the lamp, got a little bit drink, and slowly walked to the window.

Everything outside was shivering in the wind, even the curtain inside the window also seemed to tremble. Excellent sound insulation windows blocked out the noise, Hi Fi was playing Rachmaninoff 's piano concerto No.2. His eyes inadvertently past downstairs scattered shade garden, when he suddenly found a white figure next to wisteria, took a closer look, that was a beautiful oriental girl. She was alone there, it was so late now, what was she doing? ____ She was walking on the balance beam.

At this cold dark night in late fall, wind was blowing so strong, a man even shook if only stood outside, no sane man would walking around on a so high and narrow wood in the wild night, was she crazy? Or she was in a big problem of her life?

In the moment, Suraj generated an impulse, he wanted to fly to downstairs, to take the girl from the fury night and rescued her from the witch's spell, took her back to the warm safety castle. But . . . .

The girl was wearing a white sports wear, head down slightly, but her back was straight, the pensive look, her demeanor seemed to be walking in a forest, a leisurely stroll along the beach or the street. The wind was screamed, attacking the girl's body, her long black hair was flying up, but she looked neither feel cold, nor feared this devil running amok night. Every thing around her in the world was in the restless frenzy, but didn't irrelevant her calm steady walking.

In her heart, flame obviously now was shinning, grasping a fulcrum of Libra, thus made her to be the center of the world witch wanted to swallow destroy defeat. Suraj now understood, the one who need to be saved was not the girl, but himself. However, why would the girl like to be outside alone at night and in this weather? Suraj always slept late, but had never seen someone come to walk on the beam at night, during the day will be some naughty kids playing there, and one month ago, a sad man had been sitting on the beam, hanging two legs, smoked long time under the moonlight unconsciously. Suraj had stood by window near an hour, and that girl still was walking around on the balance beam. Confused and tired disturb his mind, Suraj went to get more drink, when came back to the window, the girl had gone. Suraj stood there for a long time.

The next night, around midnight, after ten hours of working, Suraj Ram logged off the computer, then came to the window.

No one downstairs, and the balance beam was covered with leaves, asleep in quiet garden.

The third day was same. He felt some sadness and ridiculous for his expectations.

It began to rain at the fourth night, also windy, the voice of rain was anxious, it seemed to crush everything.

Suraj was a night owl, 0 0'clock, he put down the music scores, turned off the light, came to the window again. But his heart was afraid to see that figure who was he looking forward to.

The girl appeared in the garden again, hold umbrella, same like that day, walking leisurely, poised herself on the balance beam gracefully, as stable as a tree. Suraj could not see the girl's face, only saw her moved two legs. Was she training her physical qualities, or trying to balance heart mind? Why did she do it? She seemed so calm, complete, and indulging in her own world, transcend worldliness and attain holiness, nothing could bother her, shake her. Suraj felt a little agitated, he thought that he must need to do something, he walked back and forth in the room, looking around, clasping his hands, but could not think of any way and meaning of action, he felt he just liked a bird in the cage. Finally he sat down by his piano, his finger started to play, a stormy came out from his hands.

Before Suraj get the answer, the girl disappeared again. However, Suraj could not get rid of that figure from his mind any more.

The snow in the end of year was also the first snow in this winter, between the night and the day, one foot of snow had cover everywhere, the center garden got makeup by jade powder. At the quiet midnight, a girl hold umbrella, slowly walked to the balance beam, she stopped, stood by the beam, she saw a white plastic folder and a red rose. Girl did not move, thought a moment, then, she carefully picked up the folder, gently brushed the top of the snow, opened it, there was actually a set of piano scores, the name of the song was <<The Ballet On The Balance Beam>> dedicate to a night elf."

Since then, Suraj Ram had never seen that elf on the balance beam again.

11

FATE

Every day at dusk, some people drove through this quiet streets, they broke before the bridge when the traffic light got red, they probably would not pay attention to an ordinary window on a six-stories apartment building beside the street, but one day, Suraj Ram saw something when his car broke at the red light, he noticed the window and the lights behind the curtain, the curtain was printed on some music notes. Since then, whenever he drove to pass here, Suraj always turned his head to recognize that the curtains and the notes. This was just out of his professional curiosity. On several times, because of he didn't move when the traffic light changed from red to be green, the car behind him horned.

In fact, Suraj Ram right lived in another apartment across the center garden with this building. Drove over the bridge, his car came down the road to other way. From the window of his apartment, could see that building opposite the center garden, but that window which was with music notes curtain was face to another direction.

A weekend in summer, it was already dark and started raining, Suraj drove to home, he got red light again before the bridge, he broke the car, then he suddenly heard a cappella female chorus. In the raining, that melody sound very soft and beautiful, Suraj felt surprised, because that voice was not radio, but real people were singing. He stared at that window with music notes, he was sure that song came from there, he held breath to listen, but he could not remember what song this was. The car behind him horned again, Suraj saw the light has changed to be green, He quickly drove down the bridge, turned into the apartment district, rushed to that apartment downstairs. He got off the car, stood in the rain, looked upward to find that window, the song was still singing, along with the rain spilled down. Suraj listened carefully, then he also identified the music notes on the curtain was the song <<You rise me up>>. Suraj Ram returned into his car, called his friend Peter Riccardo.

After 20 minutes, he reached Riccardo's house. Suraj sat in the sofa, trying to sing a part melody of that song, then asked Riccardo What song this was. Riccardo thought awhile, then said that it might be the eighteenth century composer Allegri's <<Lord chants>>." There were total nine movements in the song, very beautiful melody, and even then only be allowed to play in imperial palace, liked a royal treasure, could not be spread to the folk. But later, a royal composer heard this song when it was playing in the palace, he had remembered all nine movements, then, the song had got spread from the royal palace to the folk. This composer was just Mozart, he was only 14 years old in that year."

Suraj heard that, felt very ashamed, he was 34 years old already, have studied music for more than 20 years, even didn't know this song, and only remembered a short of it after listened.

Riccardo smiled and comforted him, said: "Mozart was Mozart after all, how many genius in the world? Mozart not only stole the Royal music to the folk, also stole heaven's music to the folk, so God early to take him back. Would you want to be back early?"

Suraj smiled and shook head said: "Yes, all the beautiful music are from God."

Riccardo then asked his wife Rosalyn to find the CD of the song and played it. Suraj identified, said: "Yes! That's right the song. Really beautiful, especially at night time listening in the rain, so pious."

Riccardo asked Suraj where did he hear of the song?

Suraj then told about that window with the music notes on curtain, and that charming female chorus. Riccardo nodded.

At 7 o'clock in the next evening, somebody rang the doorbell of Medie's apartment, the 5th girl Yu came to open the first door, and when she stood inside the security door, she saw two well-dressed gentlemen and a beautiful white lady outside. Medie then came over to ask what happened. Suraj Ram got a big surprise as soon as he saw Medie. Yu looked very surprise too at that moment, she pointed Suraj Ram and said: "Brahm, Brahms!"

Three visitors laughed. Riccardo shook head and said: "Excuse me ladies, sorry to bother your family, but my friend Brahms drives pass your apartment building down there on the bridge every day, several times almost got accident, so I' d like to solve this problem today." then he offered his business card.

Suraj Ram was also took out his card, said: "I am, Brahms 'relative', so, look a bit like him."

Medie took over their cards through the security door, look, they actually were music director and pianist of Esprit Orchestra, and the lady was their first violin.

"Ok, lady and gentlemen, welcome. But sorry, our rooms are messy right now. In the fact, we are going to move out tomorrow." Medie opened the door for them.

Riccardo whistled: "Oh, we almost missed!"

"It's a miracle." Suraj Ram thought, still looked at Medie.

"This must be a fate, just like Chinese people said." Rosalyn smiled and walked in.

But later Suraj got know, the one he saw on the balance beam in the stormy night was not Medie, but her sister Jin.

12

In Everything Give Thanks

Since Jin's family emigrated to Canada, they went to Dean's house on every weekend for ESL, they made many new friends there, and got a lot of help, also improved their English.

In the first two years, for making live, Jin and Medie did more than 10 jobs, at the most difficult time, Jin kept working overtime, had fainted and fall down at the production line. Every day after work and weekend, they persevered with music education and choir rehearsal to their children.

When the third Thanksgiving Day coming, girls had moved into a bigger government welfare apartment. Jin was hired to be art assistant of Esprit Orchestra and conductor of its chorus, Medie got her professional job too, she worked at the Life Scientific Research Central of York University now. Her inventions "Simulation Massage Robot For Home" and "Holographic Body Scan And Invisible Acupuncture Treatment Cabins" obtained a patent in Canada and in U.S.. Jin and Medie invited

Dean, Suraj Ram, Peter Riccardo and Rosalyn to their new apartment for Thanksgiving Day dinner.

Girls roasted a turkey, even though they themselves would not eat, they are vegetarians. They also prepared pasta, toast, vegetable salad, fruit, pumpkin pie and Chinese soup. During the dinner, Dean told a story to them:

"There was a boy named Will, in his 15 years old, his father sent him to his uncle's house to help them ride out the storm. It was a very far country, Will had lived there about a year. Every day, he worked at uncle's farm, Sunday, he served at the church as a volunteer, Will learned a lot. When the Thanksgiving Day, Will had to leave. In order to thank him for the help, uncle gave him some sheep, Will had to bring these sheep to home.

"It was a long way. Every night, Will and his sheep had to ask for lodging in somebody's house. To express gratitude to the owners, Will always want to take half of his sheep out to give the owner, but the next morning, when Will ready to leave, the owner gave a sheep back to Will again. Every day like so, gave half, and return one. On the day Christmas, Will finally returned to his home. Father were very happy to see him. Will brought back total four sheep. Do you know how many sheep did Will's uncle give to Will?"

This story was originally a question. Dean said that his father pastor John had asked this question to a lot of people, but most people gave up, only a few people got the answer. Some people solved it as an equation, but this was not a math question. Answer it, we all have enough IQ and EQ, because it required only a little bit of your imagination. But most importantly, we need to understand more and to learn giving love.

At this moment, Ark and five girls all hands up, said: "I know! I know!"

Dean saw it, happy and laugh, he points Ark. Ark confidently replied: "Will's uncle gave Will one pair of sheep, those owners did not want to separate them, because the ewe was pregnant, so they returned one to Will. The third and the fourth ones are baby sheep, were born on the day Christmas when Will took them home, they represent Thanksgiving."

13

THE DREAMS OF MUSIC

1

Easter long weekend, Jin and Medie were invited to come to Peter Riccardo's house for a masquerade. Actually it wasn't a party, but a music salon.

It started to rain after dinner time. Jin and Medie parked the car near a house, they was there were about ten cars had been parked in front of the house already.

The sound of piano was pouring out with the lights, the door was opened for them, a gentlemen wearing a tail coat showed out. Medie smiled as soon as she saw him, she recognized that it was Peter, he wore a mask of Franz Liszt.

"Hello! Mr. Liszt! Nice to meet you!"

"Good evening Ladies, Welcome!" Liszt politely bowed to them, took their coat, then led them came inside the hall where was a long table there.

They saw many masks on the table, all were some famous musicians' face, including female, such as violinist

Anne-Sophie. Mutter, singer Sarah. Brightman . . . . Jin selected a mask, that was French female conductor, composer and music educator Nadia Juliette Boulanger, Medie selected the mask of pianist Clara Wieck Schumann.

"I hope you will have a wonderful time tonight!" Liszt then led them to be the basement.

The lighting were little dim, whole basement were renovated very well, dark red tone, looked like a small Chamber Music Hall. More than twenty guests had seated in the brown-red sofa, every one with the mask, face to the playing area. on the left of the playing area was a black piano, an ancient Greek music sign was hanging on the wall above the fireplace, there was a 60-inch size-screen TV on the right and an excellent sound quality fever equipment, a tall shady green plants was at the corner. Behind he auditorium, all the bookcase against the wall, which has a collection of sets of various versions of the classical music CD and DVD, and music books.

Sisters seated in the last row. TV was playing an opera DVD. Jin saw that it was in September 1998, Italian festival opera house in the Imperial Ancestral Temple of the Forbidden City in Beijing staged opera "Turandot", conducted by Zubin Mehta Jin went to the scene, the ticket was from her friend, conductor Yang Li. Jin had just come back from a business trip at that time, she saw performances advertising in Beijing Subway, but tickets had been sold out. She was still grateful for Yang Li. Jin also still clearly remembered the day she saw thousands of fans excitedly came to watch the opera, as if a grand holiday, she felt so happy for the classical music.

A few years had gone, at this moment, she was living in a foreign country, deeply miss the old friends and good times.

Jin looked at another guest, she saw one looked very like Lang Lang, and even he was wearing the mask of Lang Lang. Jin knew that Lang Lang was really in Toronto now for his recital.

2

7:30, a pianist wearing Chopin' mask came in, the audience applauded immediately. Jin recognized that was Suraj, he was smiling to her behind the mask. Chopin went to the piano, like a formal performance, bowed to everyone, then sat down and started to play Chopin's Nocturne in B flat minor.

It was one of the most famous Nocturne of Chopin. The brilliance of the stars, sparkling sea shore, crystal clear, vivid, poetic, night garden, reminiscent of the night sky, feel like being on the beach under the stars. Distant, tranquil, serene, quiet, and gradually fell in sweet dreams . . . .

Music was the end in applause, Chopin stood up, one hand leaning on the piano, bowed, then he walked off the stage, sat down beside Nadia Boulanger.

"How come you like the mask of an old lady?" Suraj whispered.

"Every body will be old." Jin said, and smiled.

At this moment, they heard the sound of the moderator tonight Liszt:

"This Salon is to provide a place to showcase our music dreams to interact jointly explore, seek opportunities to achieve these dreams. Proved, some of our classical music lovers, have advance the vision even more than the professional musicians, more savvy and creativity. hopes, our dreams today, in the near future, will become a beautiful reality."

In grateful applause, Liszt handed the microphone to a guest who sat at the first row of auditorium, and then sat down by the piano.

The first speaker was wearing the masks of conductor Leonard Bernstein, he said: "Sometimes I really want to be an electronic music engineer, because I always have a dream—one day, we will see a electronic symphony concerts with all digital instruments, electronic display score, don't need to bring score, don't need to turn over the score paper, don't need the score stand, bring a small memory card, then you can see the screen of the electronic musical score."

Enthusiastic applause.

3

The next speaker was pianist Clara Schumann, she came to the front, stood beside the piano.

"Good evening everyone! May I ask all of you, who have read the book 《Water knows the answer》?"

Only a man "Seiji Ozawa" raised his hand.

"Ok, then I'd like to brief you about the relationship of water, life and music witch this book talks about."

Clara Schumann put a CD into computer, turn on the TV with a remote control, the cover of the book appears on the screen, it has Japanese, English and two Chinese editions.

"This is the information that I have downloaded from the Internet." Clara started to introduce, "Japanese Dr. Emoto Masaru is the president of the Association of Friends of the International fluctuations. Since 1994, he was in the low-temperature laboratory, using a high-speed camcorder to take photos of water crystallization. In 1999, Dr. Emoto Masaru published this book. With plenty of photographs in the book to proved a phenomenon, that is—the water is able to receive and to distinguish from voice, characters, images, music, good or evil ideas. The results was incredible, the crystallization of water are beautiful in sounding music, kind words and ideas, such as 'love', 'gratitude', the crystalline of water was broken and scattered when it was listening to rock music."

Clara Schumann changed a page of screen, a lot of photos of water crystals appeared on the screen. Guests exclaim.

"This experiment is the crystallization of pure water in glass bottles produced after listening to the different music. We all know, beautiful music has a therapeutic effect to our body, mind and spirit. What impact will produce fluctuations of the sound to the water? look at this set of photos, this is the photo of crystallization of water listening to Smetana's 'My Country', very beautiful, crystalline faithfully reproduce the beauty of the original song and the music contains the mercy of mother. And this is the crystallization of water after listening to Strauss's 'The Blue Danube', and those photos are crystallization of water when listening to Schubert's 'Ave Maria' and the movie'The Sound of Music—Edelweiss', Beethoven's 'Pastoral Symphony' and Mozart's'Symphony No. 40'. We can see, the water crystalline gorgeous, neat and vibrant. Then let's look at this picture below, this one is the water listening to heavy metal music, is full of anger and resistance to color, the shape of the crystalline, all messy and broken."

Clara Schumann put down the laser light, said: "There is 70% water in our body, there is 70% water cover the glob. Now, we understand that our life need love and gratitude, and also requires good music and wisdom. All of us here are lucky and wise, because we love beautiful music. It's not everyone is destined to know classical music. Wonderful information give an immeasurable impact to our lives, so we have to try to create and find good information to make our living environment full of wonderful music and language.

"Every kind of information is energy to us when we hear, see, smell, feeling. In Taoism, called the nature fluctuations in universe is 'Tao'; to follow this universe fluctuations is 'De', Tao and De means moral, to follow moral, the world will be harmony and stability, therefore, moral is the most perfect health of fluctuation phenomena in the universe.

"The renowned Buddhist Master Jingkong in Taiwan had been to province Shanxi in mainland China to visited a tumor hospital, he met some patients there, hospital diagnosis they were certified dead, they were ready to go home to die. Master Jingkong said to them: when you home, every day to constantly recite Amitabha, keep to do and see what happens? A few months later, these patients did not die, but miraculously recovered, superstitious? this is the result of the fluctuation in principle. chanted itself has been with the best energy, it is the best information to chanting, Buddha Bodhisattva, this is the best idea. Keep an good idea to replace thousands ideas, will be able to maintain their own physical and mental quiet good, no distractions defilements, will change the cancer cells all back to be normal. Does this mission like water? Most of our body is water, you have a bad idea, it will deteriorate, you sick; you keep good ideas, it will return to normal and health, so it is the ideas changed you, if you know the truth, insist on receiving good information, good ideas, your life will not be sick, this is true, the easiest wisdom of no sick."

Every one applauded and nodded.

Clara Schumann continued:

"In 2001, Master Jingkong established the Pure Land College in Toowoomba, Australia, in the college, teachers and students planted vegetable in garden, the vegetables are based on the traditional method of planting, never chemical fertilizers, never sprinkle pesticides. Master Jingkong said: The secret of their planting is let these vegetables and fruits and flowers and trees listen to them recite Amitabha, and listen to them every day, listen to the best information. The college in country, the vegetable garden is big, usual they supply 300 people to eat. When the good climate, will be a bumper crop, looks very beautiful and big. People at vegetables market saw that and asked: 'your vegetable grown so well, how did you planted?' They said it daily recite Amitabha, the best information, made their tissue have become the best, the juice of the fruits and vegetables are formed beautiful crystals, so everyone looks mental upright, full of life, people eat the fruits and vegetables is not easy to get sick. Chinese people said 'Good thing make people happy', when you feel happy, you laugh, it is the best time, your face look shiny, why? because your body at that moment got wonderful fluctuations and crystallization."

Everyone clap and laugh, someone stood up and shook hands with Clara Schumann to pay tribute to her. Another female pianist Martha Adelaide Ridge stood up and said:

"I suddenly have an idea—if anyone can follow these photos of water crystals to make crafts, art works, decorative in buildings, parks or home houses, or made into jewelry such as necklaces, brooches, made a gift to give to our friends and family, and to express our love and gratitude to them, not heaven-sent good thing?"

Guests applauded, smiled and said: "Great idea!"

4

That last speaker was Nadia Boulanger, her said:

"Many years ago, I had an aesthetic subject in university, called 'Aesthetics of Color-Music'. I have a dream—transform music to be colored lighting system by digital technology, synchronization convert, music control colored lighting group, colored lights performance of music in the same time, the intensity of sound, tone, pitch, rhythm and melody line—make the music becomes visible, which can be used for a variety of music recital, concert, regardless of the symphony or solo, like the London Albert Royal Concert Hall as the most brilliant, or a casual kind of like New York's Central Park amphitheater, classical music concerts or rock concert, all music fountain at city Square, anywhere need music can install this 'music-color lighting digital conversion system', including the sound system for family, as well as the music school teaching system.

"At present, in some places of entertainment, such as karaoke bars, dance halls, there are some large-scale concerts, concert, have the use of the large stage lighting system used to heighten the music atmosphere, but they are not controlled by the music, whether their scale and form are simple or complex, are artificially prepared in the program, at most, with the change of the rhythm by music, increase sensory stimulation to audience, but not in the form of color to performance of music. The 'Music-Colored Lights Digital Conversion System' I want to make it to translate music into color's language, visual language, even deaf people can also enjoy the music by the color lighting system and it is implemented by digital technology, a variety of musical works can be show in a color graphics via computer software, it also support music learning, music teaching, music composition.

"Music and color, express each other. In fact, the color music has long been a genre of music art. Chromatography and spectroscopy, sound waves and light waves, timbre and color, seven tones with seven colors, they produce a synesthesia. When you hear the "Blue Danube", they will emerge out of the wide flowing blue wave.

"In the 18th century, the great physicist Newton found that the particle nature of light, it was soon recognized that the nature of the fluctuations of the light from the white light, parse out the seven colors, red, orange, yellow, green, green blue, blue, purple. Since then, people trying to figure out the link between the law of sonic and Light wave, the most simple thing is linked the seven tones and seven colors.

"Many musicians and artists had studied and explored. Louis. Chrysler wrote a book about modern music and color. Some body had linked the sound frequency range of human ear can hear and the visible light spectrum ribbon.

"In the beginning of the twentieth century, this color musical performances is quite popular with many musicians and artists, as well as scientists for the creation and performance of this form. In 1895, Professor Farmington Figure made a 'colored organ' performances, at London's Royal College, the colored organ produced color light reflected on the above the band and piano, it accompanied the band to play the music of Chopin and Wagner. Professor Farmington Figure also wrote a book in 1911 <<The color music—The art of flow color>>.

"In the development process of the color of music, many musicians were many practical and creative, the famous ones: Alexander. Raz Luo invented 'color piano,' can play process injection color images on the screen to accompanied by the music, he is also the author of the book 《Color Light—Music》 .

"Adrian. Bernadette created a Etudes <<Color Music—light art>>, in 1913 he published <<The composition of color music>>.

"Bliss wrote <<Color Symphony>> in 1922, the movement titled were: purple, red, blue, green.

"With the rapid development of science and technology, laser technology is also applied to the color music, laser color music performances in the 1973 in Chicago Planetarium.

"American musicologist Mary Wong said: 'sound is audible color, the color is visible voice.' Every kind of music has a special emotion." Nadia Boulanger then showed every one a chart on screen, she explained:

"There are 88 keys on modern piano, from A2 to c5. By the standard a1 = 440Hz, where the sound frequency from g1 to # g2 are:

g1 #g1 a1 # a1 b1 c2 # c2
392 415.3 440 466.2 493.9 523.2 554.4

d2 # d2 e2 f2 # f2 g2
587.3 622.3 659.3 698.5 740 784

"The different frequencies of light decided it's different color, the color produced by the visible light in the following this frequency range are:

purple-red red red-orange orange orange-yellow
405 440 480 500 510
yellow yellow-green green green-blue blue blue-purple
520 530 560 600 620 650

purple purple-red red
680 790 830

"Please watch the relationship of the acoustic frequencies and wave frequency, "Nadia Boulanger said, "under this two set of members, I found off this following list."

G1 A1 # A1 B1 C
purple-red red red-orange orange orange-yellow

C D# D E F # F
yellow yellow-green green green-blue blue blue-purple

G #G
purple purple-red

"Each group of sound has twelve tones, corresponds to a group of 12 colors, from the low to be high, with the improvement of the scale, the relative brightness of the color group is also increasing at each step, 88 keys on the piano respectively corresponding to 88 different colors of lights, twelve group a cycle. In lighting system, is not only a lamp for each tone correspond to, but the vertical one set of lights, for performance of Pressure the intensity of sound."

"My sister Medie is an engineer, she helped me to design the system diagram and schematic, software and hardware, but we didn't have money to made it. After one year, I got the patent. I found out the only company witch can made this production at that time, their managers were very interested in it, signed contract with me for the cooperation and they soon really made out the sample, even they sold one set of the lights system to Korea, another one set to Singapore, after that, the company was closed, due to their internal problem. I feel so sorry, but unfortunately, until now, still no body could make it any more."

Everyone shook head. Nadia Boulanger said finally:

"I have been hoping that in my lifetime, still can see the 'music-colored lights system' one day will be set up on the top of the stage, at the concert in Central Park in New York, at the square of Toronto City Hall. I hope all of you, when one day in the evening, you leave or come to a city, when your airplane fly over the city center square, and you saw there was to hold a large-scale concert there, shining from the lighting system over and around the stage, although you could not hear the sound of the music, but it can be seen from that changing colorful lights, you would know that was Beethoven's choral symphony "Ode to Joy."

14

All Things Chorus

In the second year when Jin was hired as Art Assistant of Esprit Orchestra and conductor of its Chorus, she was invited to lead her Philharmonic Girls Band to Los Angeles, cooperated with Los Angeles Philharmonic and American scholars Choir to hold her individual concert as a special conductor. In addition to five girls, music director of Esprit Orchestra Riccardo, pianist Suraj and their first violin Rosalyn will go with Jin.

Airplane was landing in the twilight, on the way from Los Angeles airport to the hotel, their van past a magnificent concert hall, girls amazed looking at the big building through the car windows, here just would be the stage where they would show their talent, to make the dreams came to be true. Then, the 2nd girl Shang told everybody a story:

"At the turn of the last century in the United States, an artist, he was born in a peasant family, the father was Irish Canadians a child, he sold the newspaper and participated Red Cross in World War I. After the war, he returned to

Kansas City to find a meager salary working in a movie advertising companies, the most difficult time, he lived in a garage with a mouse, as partners, sometimes no money even to buy oil paints. Finally one day, the film company asked him to make a cartoon, his brains thought hard all day, and overturned numerous programs, he suddenly inspired when he saw the little mouse in the garage. Soon, he created a little mouse for a complete prototype of the world's first cartoon movie <<Mickey Mouse and Donald Duck>>. Now Disney cartoons and Disney theme park has been sweeping the world, Disney kingdom to the world of all ages people to create a colorful fantasy and innocence happiness. Mr. Disney once said: 'All your dreams can be achieved if you have the courage to pursue them.'"

Costumes, props, makeup, choreography, lighting, and the Los Angeles Philharmonic Choir, Children Choir, as well as the nation's scholars choir, the rehearsals in three days all like formal performance.

Three months ago, the advertisement on the website of Los Angeles Philharmonic Orchestra just had shown that it would be a Symphony Chorus Special Concert Conduct By Jin Qin. Before the advertisement showed out, Jin had ever put forward an idea, made Riccardo, Suraj and Mr. Raphael quite surprised—she hoped that there would be no sheet music in the concert.

"I do not want to see the sheep music shelf on the stage and hear the sound when any body turned the page of sheet," Jin said, "I hope every player and chorister prior to memorize music scores and lyrics, when they perform on stage, I want them to just look at conductor, so they can become one, to creates a real musical atmosphere. Every actor should be aware that we are inviting the audience to listen to our music, but not the audiences are inviting us to play music. The vigor from our show had embodied the connotation and denotation of the music. This embody can greatly arouse all the senses of the audience, so that they are attracted to participation and integration into the strong emotions the music played from the heart express with the atmosphere, even deaf people can see the music endoplasmic from the actions and demeanor of the band, its intensity and melody, it radiated a strong ideological and infectivity but this music creating an atmosphere not only by sound itself to achieve, why else would want to hear live it? Audience is to enter the atmosphere of this kind of music? Did they go to watch the playing techniques?"

Every body was thinking. Jin continued to say:

"Many players in the entire performance process rarely watch conductor, if no music score, their eyes just stare at their own instruments only, they put the position of score and conductor reversed. A player who can not play without score can not become a soloists. As a symphony orchestra, need to be the level of overall performance, the art of overall cooperation, to get rid of dependence on the score in spirit, liberation and detachment from form, allowing yourself to become more independence, freedom, integrity, we will not only played, but also to reach the realm of the second creation, totally into the mastery of music and explain. In some concerts, the sheets shelves are not placed neatly enough, neither respect for the audience, nor respect for the music my band I want to look at conductor, the conductor to unify, coordinate and mobilize their momentum, in order to make their breath more closely together. Performance of the eyes are very important in the theatrical arts, is one of the qualities of the actor. We are not only there to play music, but also during stage performances, eyes, facial expression, body posture, these mental outlook are elements of theatrical arts, directly formal beauty of the performance, convey the thoughts and feelings of the music. No sheets music, no action to turn the sheets, stage performances will not clutter does not interfere with the visual of the audience, the audience will be able to better understand the music itself.

"The whole orchestra watch conductor, just like one person is breathing, as if the whole orchestra and chorus is a musical instrument in conductor's hands, will produce an intense and captivating magnetic field radiation, the inner spirit and breath of the music to the audience, like bake bread, surrounded them, ignite them with fire enthusiasm, within minutes they bake cooked by the emotion of the music, the band and the audience into a pair of couples climax lover, this is our ultimate goal."

Everyone was persuaded eventually by her, thus, in accordance with the requirements of the Jin, the orchestra would no scores shelf, all chorus members would also unarmed debut, whole concert would be paperless, Jin would catch the attention of everybody, to weave their musical soul.

Tonight, Walt Disney Concert Hall that was located at the intersection of First Street and Grand Avenue in the City of Los Angeles would be no empty seats, all tickets were sold out, nearly half audiences were Chinese. American Vegetarian Association, the organizers of the concert, which co-organized and sponsored groups for some viewers to feel curious and puzzled.

Walt Disney Concert Hall has experienced 16 years of ups and downs, and was able to completed construction in October 20, 2003. This large ultra-modern building with its unique appearance captivating become a new landmark in the second largest city of Los Angeles, has also become art galleries and music lovers and tourists are common worship.

Under the summer sun irradiation, concert hall silver stainless steel housing shiny, so that it eclipsed slightly gray and dull high-rise buildings around. Every witness the building for the first time all who feel the eyes suddenly light up their amazement.

The idea of the construction of the Walt Disney Concert Hall was first proposed by Mrs. Disney, in 1998, the master architect Gehry beating many opponents, with its innovative and avant-garde design in one fell swoop Championship. The whole building total project cost of $274 million, which lasted four years. The stage behind the design of a 12-meter-high giant floor-to-ceiling windows for natural light the daytime concerts as held in the open, out the window of pedestrians passing also enjoyed playing in concert halls, indoor and outdoor blend, this design unique. Frank Gehry, in order to express his admiration for Mrs. Disney, specially roses theme designed concert hall back garden, because the Disney Lady during his lifetime favorite white roses he sent.

Who was the protagonist of this evening? Jin designed four sets of costumes for five girls—The first set was Chinese cheongsam skirt of silk fabrics, on the front, respectively printed on Chinese "Gong, Shang, Jiao, Zhi, Yu" in five colors, with glitter exposure to the waist, back to oval, lined a translucent tulle and silk fabrics with colors above were printed on "gold, wood, water, fire, earth", the performance of the five-color, Pentatonic, the five elements of the Chinese culture, its style, both classical and avant-garde, was a sub-wear the proud design, completely hand-refined. Blue purple and pink intertwined under the stage lights. The concert was started in a beautiful female quartet <<Butter fly Lovers>>, the 2nd girl Shang played violin, while gently walking at the symphony orchestra to other four sisters. Audience immediately broke into enthusiastic applause, and respond to that issue from the mind of the Millennium. The next, girls sang <<Pastoral>> (a cappella) and <<Silk Road> (Jin played Guqin, the 3rd girl Jiao plays Chinese bamboo flute to accompany).

When Jin conducted Los Angeles Philharmonic and scholars choir to sing the famous <<Chorus of the Hebrew slaves>> of Verdi's opera <<Nabucco>>, girls exited. The first half of the tracks were more lightweight, elegant, Jin did not use the baton, unarmed conduct by her hands and arms and finger movements delicate head and waist dance language more elegant and expressive beauty, the chorus of her hands, as if pieces of exquisite musical instruments, and any of her acting freely. She wore a dark blue short dress, thin waist, bright long hair, steady sight. People tasted of her style through music, including every detail of her, as if she was a leader of the neo-classical fashion models. The audience would soon find that scores shelf stage, regardless of the symphony orchestra, chorus or conduct himself, there would be no paper on the stage. Tonight, Jin would seize the attention of all the actors and the audience, refining their musical soul.

For the most audience, this was the first time to see a paperless concert, many people praise: "Wonderful! It's fabulous!"

After girls came back on the stage again, they had changed the second set of costumes—Chinese style silk suit in light-colored with embroidered pine, orchid, plum flowers, bamboo and chrysanthemum. With orchestra accompaniment, girls and scholars Choir sang large-scale choral works composed by Jin—<<Universe Zen>>, <<Inter-star Through>>, <<Grand Canyon>>, and <<China fantasy symphonic choral—Snow Mountain. Shangri La, Three Gorges, Terra-cotta And Warriors Of Qin Shi Huang, Taishan Mountain and The Great Wall>>. Jin extensively used many variety of percussion instruments. There was no lyrics in the chorus, Jin used vocals as an instrument, all the pronunciation was for harmony, according to her aesthetic philosophy, music was the language of the universe, all creatures can understand and enjoy. Jin's music had a far-reaching temporal and spatial sense, mystery religious sense, color contrast, a dramatic contrast of movement and stillness, movie background sense of the picture, super strong and weak rhythm contrast grasp the sense of melody, beautiful and exciting, in some section, even only used pure percussion and chorus, made audience surprised, everyone's palms sweating, every nerve was beat with the music.

She was a great musician. Suraj was thinking, he sat at back left side on the stage by his piano, looked at Jin. He had started to worship her, fell in love with her before they knew each other, since that night, on that balance beam.

But Jin didn't know it, Suraj had been thinking that when and how to let Jin knew that he loved her.

The next song was <<Meditation in the varicolored world>>, Jin composed and played Guqin, the 3rd girl Jiao played bamboo flute to accompany, other four girls sat down at the rear of stage to performance meditation and humming wordless song, Medei wore a light blue Chinese silk clothing to play Tai Chi sword, while the big electronic screens at the both side of the stage showed Chinese landscape and calligraphy works on. Song planning immediately to win the great interest and appreciation of the audience, some of the ethnic Chinese Tai Chi audience even gestured to follow up on the seat. On the big screen this time showed some eyebrows white hair longevity elderly Chinese people play Tai Chi in the park, also some foreign students were studying in the Wu Dang Mountains; Then it was at the opening ceremony in Beijing Asian Olympic Games in 1990, fifteen hundred Chinese and Japanese Tai Chi Boxing enthusiasts performances, 1998, Tian An Men Square, thousands people played Tai Chi at the spectacular; and the film of Tai Chi of Beijing Olympic bid promo in "Eight minutes in Athens" by famous movie director Zhang Yi Mou.

Tai Chi, outside looks like a virgin, within looks like King Kong. Fitness, health, martial and Martial Arts Mercy aesthetic standpoint, Tai Chi practical and ornamental across time and space, it has an irresistible charm. Bold and creative music choral art form as Tai Chi, a ranking loudly from remote hold the audience to the stage the wonderful performance with heartfelt admiration and applause.

When the choir showed again on the stage, girls exited in applause. Then Jin conducted symphony orchestra and chorus to play Wagner's opera <<Tannhauser: Pilgrims' Chorus>>.

After that, girls came back, changed to be a group of Western-style silk strapless dress, on being tight heart-shaped embroidery around the chest, the lower part of the body A word-wide skirt with glitter and waist ribbon, the colors on the shallow depth, were sky blue with sapphire blue, emerald green with dark green, light red with rose red, apricot with orange, lotus purple with royal purple, light gray with silver gray, the young yellow with golden.

Girls sang Elgar's <<Holy Spirit>>, Barber's <<Agnus Dei>>. Then was Bach fast-paced <<Double Violin Concerto>> adaptation of the mixed chorus, several scholars Choir Boys join, the orchestra's drummer Daniel and percussionist was standing next to the small chorus accompany with shaker and tambourine.

Chorus clear and patchwork harmony skills unanimous praise from the audience as "absolutely fabulous".

The next song was <<The Deaf Musician >> (Jin adapted), girls chorus and whole choir together using only lip-silent to sing, Jin conducts, Medie stood near by Jin using hands language to interpretation of the lyrics to audiences, big screen while showed pastoral scenes screen and symphony orchestra playing Beethoven's Pastoral Symphony. The planning of this piece had touched all viewers of the site, people understood the creation of the first great works of Masters Beethoven's mood in deaf, the end, violent issued a tsunami of applause and cheers in the audience.

During the intermission, Suraj Ram sat alone in the seat reading the propaganda materials which was at the back of Manu, and he saw that there were some other viewers also were reading, but Suraj read particularly careful, because this propaganda materials were wrote by Jin, he always wanted to know her more.

Do you know, that people's everyday eating habit is bit by bit affecting the meltdown of the Iceland, fire in California, tsunami in southern Asia, poverty and starvation in Africa . . .

Human livestock activities have been more than ten thousand years, but it is only within the most recent fifty years that we have dramatically increased the supply and demand. Annual consumption of over one billion hogs, 1.3 billion cattle, 1.8 billion goats and 15.4 billion chickens together increased greenhouse gas emissions by 20%. On top of that, they produce 13 billion tons in waste, damaging earth, water and air quality. Cattle alone produce 18% of global CO2 emissions, more than automobiles exhaust.

Rainforests in Central and South America have been destroyed because rearing beef cattle for production Hamburg or plant soybeans for feeding animals. These damages are irreversible on a short-term and will directly affect our own living planet. If all of this pollution continues, our planet will overwhelm. In order to satisfy endless cravings and greed, we have damaged our environment to a critical point.

Carnivorousness may increase obesity, high blood pressure, heart disease, diabetes, stone, joint pain, cancer, etc. Direct and indirect treatments for related illnesses are causing global medical expense to rise rapidly. Many countries have the television specialized channel of weight loss programs, and many people are fighting hard every day with their bucket waist.

The continuing role of the tranquilizers, antibiotics, hormones, together with up to 2700 other fertilizing chemicals are fed to animals to increase their size and growth rate unnaturally. These procedures are conducted before the livestock are born. The same chemicals continue to exist in the product long after the animal is butchered, until you ate the meat. These procedures and chemicals are not required by law to be shown on product packaging.

In the United States, 90% of the cattle in captivity have been injected with hormones. Female breast cancer rate in the United States was 45% higher than the European women; male reproductive system cancer rate was two times of European, the hormone you ate from meat very likely is the reason causing these cancers.

After the nuclear explosion in Japan during the Second World War, only a very few cattle and goats were not affected by the radiation. Research found that their herbivorous diet contributed greatly to the anti-radiation nature of their bodies. It seemed that a vegetarian diet was one of the most effective Armour against the disaster.

Every nutrient human need can be found from plant food. Strict vegetarians have been confirmed to have rich antioxidants, higher immune systems and anti-aging properties.

Our personalities and moods are directly affected by the food we eat. Different food produce different chemicals and hormones that goes in our bloodstream and changes our psychological behaviors. Over time, our repeating eating habit will make the food we eat to be a part of our personalities, we are almost what we eat. A healthy body is from healthy food.

> "Earth can meet the needs of all, but can not meet everyone's desires."
>
> —Gandhi

> "All the arguments to prove that the human is superior can not change this fact: animals, like humans can feel pain."
>
> —Peter Singh

Chickens and other farm birds are often killed during times of flu virus outbreak. Related diseases killed more than 150 million farm birds. These birds are usually beaten to death, suffocated with plastic bags, burnt, CO2 poisoned, etc.

Carnivorous behavior is the most oppressive and most widely institutionalized violence on animals. We exert oppression, exploitation, plunder, violence on animals, our mutilation and massacre caused tremendous suffering and catastrophe to them, we absolutely lost moral to animals.

> "Those who abuse animals would not treat humans better."
>
> —Immanuel Kant

> "Compassion is the basis of any moral necessary, to embrace all of life is not limited to humans, would reach its most complete depth and breadth."
>
> —Albert Schweitzer

> "Animals in the world are not created for human, just like black man is not created for white man, women are not created for men."
>
> —Alice Walker

1/3 of the world food productions go to 13 %of the population. Canada and the U.S. have 5 % of the world's population, but consume 18% of world's food production and mostly used for feeding livestock.

In some African countries, starvation is still a big problem. Be food resources world not scarce but equally distribution.

A pound of meat require on average 16 pounds of corn, wheat and other feeds. Having a vegetarian diet not only stand on a morality but is of huge benefit to the environment, to liberate the land that is used to feed those poor animals.

> "We can neglect our rights and power but we cannot forget our responsibilities to sustain the environment for our own future generations. This will be a shame and failure of the human race."
>
> —Ananda Moody

God created all things in existence like parents have their children, some are smarter, and some are less so. If a smarter child tells his parents that he would like to kill his brother or sister for being less wise, would the parents agree?

Vegetarianism is actually a spiritual revolution, the declaration of spirit, and no longer sinks into the abyss of substance.

"No harm that is the highest of the law."
—"Mahabharata"

Islam: Animal fats will increase beastliness, beastliness will dominate spirituality. Vegetarian diet helps cleanse the body and improve spirituality; it's health and moral lifestyle.

Muslim Sufi poet has once described carnivorous behavior to be the loss of love and moral. Even being with others whom killed for food is a pollutant to the mind. What we need to kill is our lust, greed, pride and ignorance, rather than the other animals.

Thai vegetarian movement's leaders, many of them are devout Buddhists, and, at the same time, the medical profession or spiritual authority, Thailand vegetarian Center founder Doctor S Kosolkitcoong had compared vegetarian diet and meat diet, he said:

"Meat from animals is lower level food, because the meat is the sources of lust, anger, in essence, it is dirty.

"The predator inevitably absorb a lot of pain, because the meat is often the product of long-term suffering, bloodshed, tears, full of fraud, exploitation and injustice. Carnivorous human body has become the world's largest tomb, filled with desires of selfishness and dirty, buried countless innocent lives.

"Vegetarian is the finest food, because they come from pollen dispersal blessing after the essence of sun and the moon, clean and pure.

"Meat is obtained with brutal force and cruel methods from sentient being sits master was by no means willing to be killed, butchered, barbecue or cooking inevitably resist to death, full with bloody, even after death, their grief anger is still not lost, and will continue to worry the killers and people who eat them. "

Meat consumption is harmful to both the body and the mind. Vegetarians are gentle and calm, their blood flows smoothly, body refreshing, energetic, more patience, their minds filled with compassion, kindness, peace and love, co-existing in harmony with the nature. This promotes them to live a longer life. A from the Tang Dynasty monk master Zhaozhou lived for 150 years, and modern monk master XuYun lived for 120 years.

> "Any disease out there, physically or mental, can be healed or lightened with a vegetarian diet and consumption of pure water."
>
> —Shelley

> "Future medical doctors will no longer require medicines to treat their patients, but use humane care, food control, disease prevention measures to replace."
>
> —Thomas Edison

> "When those animals know that they will be caught, be slaughtered, to be ate, we could see the pain from their expression, dejected, with tears. What is different with humankind? we really have eyes but no see, have ears but no hear, have hearts

> but no feelings, arbitrarily slaughtered them to satisfy our appetite."
>
> —Master Jingkong

A part of the human dignity is: give up meat in its gradual improvement in the process. When we lost mercy and compassion to all beings, we would lose compassion too to our own countrymen they.

It is not weakness to sympathize the suffering of others. When public is turning a blind eye, your mercy has followed your heart and action, it needs more courage and strength than compared to follow brutality of others.

Vegetarian help to repair ourselves, our planet, as well as the relations between us and the natural, saving more natural resources for our next generation.

Creatures are equal, all life has dignity, and even the deceased has dignity too. Vegetarian away from the killing, compassion growth, make countless sentient life far away from frightened, abuse, slavery, exploitation, torture, and other pain. if you want to reconstruct a paradise which God created on the earth, come to become a vegetarian, a participant of animal liberation movements. This change of course needs to take time, but our planet is looking forward to your choice.

Suraj was deep in thought after read.

The second half of the show began. Symphony orchestra and chorus re-took the stage, but the audience found the choir members actually all were men. The audience was quiet again, on the stage and everyone was waiting for their female conductor.

The gate at the corner of stage was opened, Jin finally walked out in the eyes of all look forward in applause. She changed a garment, white silk blouse was tied in black pants, long hair looked like a blue waterfall, bright as a mirror, as if each hair silk has music note. And audiences saw there was a baton in her right hand, liked a silver sword out of casket. Most people had never seen that a female conductor dressed like a man so strolled on the stage, the audience bursts issued the surprised applause and cheers. Jin stepped on the podium, hold the gold railing, sight was steady, with self-confident and smile, then bowed to the audiences in applause.

<<Polovtsian Dances>>, it was the most famous music from Borodin's opera "Prince Igor", the 12-minute song was full of the amorous feelings of foreign country. Jin conducted orchestra while sang the song with chorus together, her graceful posture captured the hearts of all the audience.

People also realized at this time that the tracks in the second half would have a male intensity color, Jin's garment effect to make up for the weaknesses of a female conductor stature thin. At the same time, the audiences also praised the artistic planning of Jin put the feminine eastern music and western masculine charm in a chorus concert.

The next track was a men's chorus by scholars Choir, whether black men, white men or Asian, whole chorus sang the song in Chinese, it was Yue Fei's "Man Jiang Hong", the other choristers vocal accompaniment, which made the audience all ethnic Chinese audience surprised, many people passionately followed chorus to sang, so Jin turned around, conducted up and down stage, and she also sang with everyone. Applause and cheers exploding, the audiences stood up, a lot of people shouting: "Bravo!

Bravo!" Jin led the chorus, bowed to the audiences again and again.

Medie and girls re-took the stage, they had changed a white silk dress, with the choir together to sing Mozart's "Jupiter Symphony, the first movement, adapted by Jin. Jin also adapted many instrument music works to be polyphonic cappella choral, the following songs just selected from the section of Paganini Violin Concerto, Beethoven's Violin Concerto, Tchaikovsky and Brahms violin concertos in D major, Albinoni's "Adagio". Medie played piano, the 3rd girl Jiao played flute to accompany.

Then, girls and scholars Choir sang together with symphony orchestra "The Champions", drums played loud and strong, energetic and high-spirited, the percussionist Daniel Davis outstanding performances also won the applause and cheers of the audience.

The next song <<Blind Musician>>, it was a wordless song by Jin adapted from Beethoven's "Moonlight Sonata" in 24-hours blackout night in North America in two years ago, when they sang this song, the lights of audience were turned off, the screen of stage background was on, moonlight spreading ballast boundless silver shiny, reflecting sleep silky undulating blue lake. Four girls stood on the stage, Medie and another girl stood on the upstairs at the corner behind the auditorium, the superb acoustics of Walt Disney Concert Hall showed wonderful reverb.

The next track was the CLS (coloratura)part of tonight show—"All Things Chorus", it was a voice symphony Jin made specifically for this concert, would be 280 people to sing, and it was also the last track of the formal performance.

All the members of the choir took to the stage, Medie and five girls still stood at cantor position. Jin stood on the podium, she turned around, facing to the auditorium, arms crossed on the front, hand pinching a baton. Behind her, every player of symphony orchestra on the stage actors and chorus were also was looking at the auditorium, looked solemn, seemed was waiting for something. At this moment, the two channels of the door behind auditorium were silently opened, the two choirs actor respectively silently walked into the venue from both sides of the aisles were filled channel on the steps with the stage on the back and both sides of the upstairs auditorium. Treble Choirs players, they wore a variety of clothing, dressed into a variety of animals and birds and fish and insects. All audiences eagerly looked forward to.

Jin stood on the stage, all eyes were turned to her now, the audience quiet, quiet as if only Jin one was here, at this moment, she became a center of quiet. Into the hearts of the people in this quiet into a beyond earthly holy distant cosmic gas field, it was a tranquility of heart and one mind, a broad and deep and eternal silence, the quiet was also music, and it was music essential background.

Suraj looked at Jin, the lady who had walked on the balance beam at dark night in the storm, she was so strong, but also so quiet. What was she thinking right now, she was so calm to stand on the podium, no audience could see that an unparalleled storm would outbreak under her baton.

Finally, Jin turned back, she slowly raised her arms, the musicians on the stage immediately found their own place. Hold breath in one second, two seconds, silver baton in the air, a flash, the thunder of drums Suddenly interpretation of a spectacular storm flood Earth wowed the audience and the orchestra and chorus, the audience felt like turned upside down as the music from their heads, the foot of the front and behind all directions coming tsunami-like rushing away.

The musical story was from Bible, Genesis, God used forty days to flood all evil on the Earth. World was corrupt before God, the God said to of Noah, a righteous man: "all flesh, his end has come before me, because the earth is filled with their violent, I want them and the earth to destroy . . . . To make the flood boom abuse on the ground, to destroy all . . . . you want to build an ark, you and your family into the ark where there are living creatures of every kind of two, a male and a female, you bring into the Ark, good preservation of life . . . ." Noah did, after all the fountains of the great deep split open the windows of heaven were opened, forty days and nights of heavy rains on the ground. The high hills, that were under the whole heaven, were covered, where the ground all kinds of living creatures were destroyed, leaving only Noah and those with him in the ark. The waters prevailed upon the earth an hundred and fifty days. After the heavy rain stopped, the water receded from the earth, the top of the hill comeback. Noah released a dove, pigeons back, the mouth and a new olive leaf. The whole year, and again did God called Noah and his family, and all the living creatures out of the ark, and call them on the ground teem mightily. Noah set up the altar to the LORD, God made a covenant with them, he will not again curse the ground because of man, all flesh not flood extinction. Whoever sheds the blood, harm to life, whether beast or person, God will avenge his sins to brothers. God put the rainbow in the clouds, the sign of the covenant as he and the earth.

The music initially rapid rhythm, melody tumbling Sharp wins and engaging. Scene after the flood days, the sound gradually stop down, quiet lasted ten seconds, a wet faintly audible sound came from distant water surface, birds scared Touch undecided. The sky cleared, the side of the stage behind the two-story auditorium sounded this time a group of minor female voice singing, later, another group of female sang beautiful lyrical theme melody strings, piano accompaniment snare drum and triangle; Next part of a group of choral color joined, joined a group band part, no lyrics, Treble chorus of children to simulate a variety of animal sounds. Finally, the whole band and chorus team theme tune to a climax, after the radical drums, music horizon sacred bell tune.

No applause, although many viewers wanted to leap into the sky, but did not indicate track single, the song was not finished, there was another part, so the audience had to fist, calmly waiting for.

More than ten seconds after a very quiet excessive, the symphony orchestra played while the idyllic leisurely broad background music, that was the beauty of the kingdom of heaven, was life in the Garden of Eden.

Long, dramatic pause a percussion performance, different color compared to the string part of many tear staggered dissonance apparent. The audience saw the text messages in English and Chinese showed on the electronic screen of both sides at the stage:

"In the Bible, Genesis, God, Adam and his wife are not allowed to kill any of the animals, their meat as food, they can only be together food all over the floor of fruits and vegetables in the Garden of Eden and Paradise killings. Destroy the world big floods before the advent of humans eating vegetarian, their life span is usually measured in centuries but after the flood, the people began to kill abuse animals and eat their flesh, initially at the altar and the temple burnt offerings, then gradually developed into a daily diet, until today's global large-scale industrialized meat market economy."

Part chorus joined in, to simulate a variety of animal sounds, images and text displayed on the big screen, along with the music began to show animals to human hunting, confinement, captivity, slavery, or used for entertainment or large-scale farms and plant breeding, artificial breed. Some of these animals had never seen a sunrise and sunset, all day stayed in the crowded and polluted the space, waiting for death in the infinite terror, and ultimately, they were slaughtered, butchered, and the body was skinned, flesh split, frozen, or hinge into the meat, processed into sausage or canned meat, sent to the market, or cooked in a restaurant and human private kitchen and backyard barbecue, human chopping block; chicken got the plague were buried alive in mass graves burned alive; human killed the baby seals in front of the seals mother; the worse is that human cut alive animals, roast alive, boil alive, eat alive those animals alive tortured death, the human stomach cemeteries and cemetery of those innocent animals; there are some animals in the human laboratory tortured, their screams very piercing, and could not bear to see.

The music stopped, the period of deathly silence, was the most important part of this song—in order to let people hear the voice of their conscience at this moment—some people cried in the dark.

Appears on the screen when the music sounded again, a clear picture—blue sky, endless ocean, green mountains, flowers, lush pastures, the vast nature, fishes, birds, species of animals enjoy their home, and everything was in harmony. Beautiful music made people felt comfortable, lovely picture of a variety of animals to show in front of people, the entire home planet peaceful and beautiful, full of vitality.

At this time, some information was showed on the electronic screen:

Some famous vegetarians in history ____
Ancient Greece: Plato, Socrates, Pythagoras,
Ancient India: Sakyamuni
Ancient Rome: Philosopher and dramatist Seneca, Poet Ovid, Writer Plutarch
The ancient Spanish: Jesus Christ
Ancient China: Lao Tzui, Confucius, Mencius
Chinese ancient king: Emperor LiangWu
The small Catholic Brotherhood founder of St. Francis
Branch Founder of the Salvation Army Booth
Protestant Wesleyans one of the founders of Wesleyan
Italy: Renaissance poet Petrarch, the painter and scientist Leonardo da Vinci
UK: poet and statesman John Milton,
Poet Shelley,
Writer Shakespeare,
Writer and historian Wales,
Poet and satirist Alexander Pope,
Playwright George Bernard Shaw,
France: writer Voltaire,
Philosopher and writer Rousseau
Germany: composer and theater Wagner,
Musician Albert Schweitzer

Russia: writer Tolstoy
United States: Authoress Alcott, Essayist and
Poet Henry David Thoreau,

Writers, journalists, inventors, democratic, politician and scientist Benjamin Franklin,
Poet Ralph Waldo Emerson,
Novelist Sinclair,
Movie actor Paul Newman,
Black comedian Dick Gregory
Singer and songwriter Bob Dylan,
Astronaut James Owen
Indian nationalist leader and advocate of nonviolence
Mahatma Gandhi
British Princess Diana and Prince Charles
Myanmar former Prime Minister U Nu

Vegetarians Who won Nobel Prize:
Tagore : 1913 Literature Prize
Albert Einstein: 1921 Physics
George Bernard Shaw:1925 Literature
Sir C. V. Raman: 1930 Physics
Albert Schweitzer: 1952 Peace
Linus Pauling: 1954 Chemistry, 1962 Peace
George Wald: 1967 Medicine
Isaac Bashevis Singer:1978 Literature
Chandrashekar Subrahmanyam: 1983 Physics
Elie Wiesel: 1986 Peace
Aung San SuuKyi: 1991 peace
V. S. Naipaul: 2001 Literature
JM Coetzee): 2003 Literature

Outstanding scientist and inventor
Sir Isaac Newton: Father of physics
John Ray: Father of British naturalist
Leonardo Da Vinci: Architect, inventor and artist
Thomas Edison: Inventor

Nikola Tesla: Inventor, physicist and engineer
Srinivasa Ramanujan: Mathematician
Edward Witten): Physicist, string theorists
Brian Greene: Physicist and string theorist
Jane Goodall: Primatologists
Vijay Raj Singh: Physicists in Medicine
Kalpana Chawla: NASA space pilot
Steve Jobs: Founder and CEO of Apple Computer

Children chorus were on and off stage, dressed into a variety of cute animals, hand in hand, the music at this time was showing various styles of beautiful dance animism the roots of all things, the harmony of all things, the wonderful picture of all things choral, the entire orchestra with all chorister, invested the various sounds of nature are intertwined, filled with prayers and blessings for the future, and the momentum is growing agitation drums, music.

The audiences stood up, applause had been unable to express their inner feelings, some people wiped tears, some people went to the front of the stage flowers to Jin, some ones were sitting in the audience of the channel next moved to embrace small chorus of players around them. Some people were sitting motionless, thinking in the continuous applause and cheers. Jin led the whole orchestra stood up and bowed to the audience.

No one wanted to leave, applause was calling Jin, she twice came back to the stage, and finally had to encore.

The first song of Encore track was the episode in the American movie <<Sister Act>>—the fast-paced distinctive, passionate and confidence, "I will follow him" the stage chorus players from both sides to the middle of the side turned singing and jumped, by the applause of the audience and beat someone drunkenly were singing together. In the end, the auditorium boiling up again, the applause was deafening.

The second song of encore track was Orff's <<O Fortuna>>, modern style accompaniment, the musical form of rhythm, forceful tunes from weak crescendo until the drums masterpiece, all released, liked an avalanche of momentum just liked invincible million lion triumphant. When the last note finished in Jin's hands, the audience mad camel leaps the rallying cheers for the superb performances of the artists. They didn't know that the young artist had such a superb artistic skills, the best in the world.

Prolonged applause, even the musicians on stage with the choir players also applauded, Jin had once again returned to the stage, conducted chorus and orchestra play the last track "You raise me up", to thanks for the love of the audience.

> When I am down, and, oh, my soul, so weary,
> When troubles come, and my heart burdened be,
> Then, I am still and wait you in the silence,
> Until you come and sit awhile with me.
> You raise me up, so I can stand on mountains;
> You raise me up to walk on stormy seas;
> I am strong when I am on your shoulders;
> You raise me up to more than I can be.

Sincere, soulful singing impressed all those present, the audience humming, some ones tears running. This was a spiritual baptism. People knew these artists spreading ballast for tonight's performance and tremendous effort put all their soul, including this concert hall, there were those lucky and lovely children. For this reason, they were grateful for the tender care of God, and praised of the glory of God. Countless flowers, hugs and kisses flew to the stage.

Jin's dignified smile was more showing her profound artistic accomplishment and temperament demeanor as a conductor.

Thank soulful expression of the Los Angeles Philharmonic musicians, girls gave flowers to them. Jin's friend percussion minister Daniel Davis humorously hugged her and said: "I feel so sorry didn't see captain Noah this time."

"I hope next time." Jin thanked him again.

At this moment, Suraj stood beside Peter Riccardo, he shook head while clapping, said: "She made a splendid concert, she conquered all tonight."

"Yah, specially you." Riccardo smiled.

"Yah, I'm the first one."

The Applause from up and down of the stage merged into one. The curtain was slowly falling in paradise cheers.

15

THE FIRST TIME INTIMATE CONTACT WITH CHINA

1

Have been to Canada more than three years already, Jin and Medie finally have saved enough money, decided to take kids back to China in this summer, visit family and by the way to a tour, let kids to see and study Chinese history, culture of five thousand years, to read the book without words. Jin said to them, as a Chinese, descendants living abroad, this would be a remedial, and also a necessary learning.

When Suraj Ram heard about this, he asked Jin: "How long will you take your vacation?"

Jin said: "Four weeks."

"That's so long."

Jin looked at him, then smiled: "But our boss said ok."

"Oh!" Suraj shook head, "I don't mean that."

Since Jin came to Esprite Symphony Orchestra, to be Suraj's colleague, Suraj got changed. Before he was weak, always sick, headache, his stomach got problem for 20 years already. Jin said, he lived alone, and didn't know how to take care himself. Jin always gave Suraj some Chinese medicine, every week cooked congee, brought to work for him, especially millet congee, Jin said that millet congee would be very good for him, his stomach had too much gastric acid. Jin told him don't eat spicy food, deep fried food, hard and cold food, no alcohol, even stop coffee and soda drink, always drink warm water, keep body warm. Jin also gave Suraj some Chinese Herb medicine and acupuncture, she used vacuum cups to do acupuncture for him.

Jin said that Medie and her had been learning Traditional Chinese Medicine, they have six kids. She showed Suraj the all acupuncture points and meridian on human body, taught him to do self massage. After three months, Suraj Ram changed to be very good, no more problem. But he still keep to eat congee, he learned Chinese Tai Chi sword from Jin, in Chinese new year, he went to Jin's apartment to eat dumplings and rice ball soup, Duan Wu Festival, Jin invited him for Zong Zi dinner, and Moon festival, he share moon cake with Jin's family. Suraj's health and emotional dependence on Jin, just like a baby. He called Jin "angel", he tried to help her family, he became to be every body's friend in this special family. So one day, Peter Riccardo asked Suraj:

"Can you live without Jin?"

"Surely I can, but, I don't want to." Suraj said.

Peter smiled, and said: "Well, let her know."

Right now, Suraj looked at Jin, then asked her carefully:

"Would you like me go to China with you?"

Jin looked at him, then smiled.

"Thanks! Angel." At that moment, Suraj really wanted to kiss her, every time when Jin brought congee and Chinese medicine for him, Suraj just wanted to hug and kiss her.

But Peter Riccardo had reminded him: "Don't rush. She's Chinese, Chinese is very implicit."

Suraj himself knew it very clearly that he had fell down into love with Jin, but he was not sure that if Jin loved him too or not, she was nice to every body, and also, there was a biggest obstacle between them.

Peter called his wife Rosalyn as soon as Suraj told him that he would like to take vacation, travel to China with Jin's family, to visit Jin's hometown, to learn more about Chinese culture.

At last, Peter and Rosalyn also joined them.

"This is our first time intimate contact with China." Rosalyn said, "It's wonderful!"

"Wow! Total eleven people!"

"We can be a tour group now."

"And we can sing songs on airplane."

Kids were more excited. Jin asked every body: "Please bring your music instrument to the travel." Then, Jin called China international travel company, said, her family wanted to be a tour group, and she need a tour guide and a bus.

Then one day, Jin put a map of China on the table to show every body, she marked circles on some place on the map, said: "Friends, we are going over there."

2

Shanghai.

From the airport to Hotel, they take magnetically levitated train, speed over 430 km/h, every body excited and takes the video.

When three friends were sitting in the revolving buffet restaurant which was on the Oriental Pearl TV tower with Jin, the skyscrapers and varicolored night view of Shanghai attracted them. But Medie took children to somewhere else for dinner. Three foreigners feel sorry about it, hope can be together with them, they will pay for them. But Jin said:

"It's not about money, it's about our faith. We are vegetarians."

They saw that only small amount of vegetables in Jin's plate, Rosalyn asked her: "Jin are you not hungry?"

Jin smiled, said: "In fact, I usually don't eat dinner. For health's sake, I'd like to let my body rest at nigh time. Some Buddhist and Taoist practitioners even only eat a little bit in a few days, can keep body more clean, it's called Bigu."

"Wow! How can live like this?"

Jin: "Yes, and they can live longer, they can get nutrition and essence from fresh air when they sit in meditation."

"It's incredible!"

Jin: "If you guys are interested in it, later you can go internet to read something about it. Ark was reading the book 《Brain and Zen》, 《Body Mind Balancing》, maybe you can share later."

"Great, I will read them." Suraj said.

When they started dinner, Jin made a pre dinner pray.

Rosalyn asked her: "Jin you are practicing Zen, how come belief in God, too?"

Jin smiled, said: "To me, they are different ways, but go o the same destination, through them, I learn meditation, humility and gratitude."

Three people nodded.

"I am more interested in Meditation now," Suraj said again, "Jin, could you tell me why you sit in meditation every day for?"

"For cleaning my mind." Jin smiled, "We take showers every day to clean our body, right? But that's only for our skin, how can you clean your body in side? There are much garbage even toxin in our body, so, I eat crude fiber food and drink pure water to clean it. Then, we cleaned our body, how can we clean our heart? We listen to the music, enjoy art works, go into nature, read Bible, and sit in meditation."

Three people nodded.

"But how to clean your mind?" Rosalyn asked.

"Just don't think about anything." Peter said.

"That's hard," Suraj said, "I had tried, but, I can't help myself, my mind always move, run to somewhere, otherwise I will be asleep."

They laughed.

"It's Kong Fu." Jin said.

Suraj then thought of a question, asked Jin: "Why need to be in that posture when meditation?"

"It's a good question. "Jin said," Well, when you closed your hands, legs, eyes and sit in a quiet place, your consciousness and feeling not contact the outside anything, it's most beneficial for you to enter the Zen static. This posture makes the body to form like a pyramid structure, which is the most stable."

"Pyramid?"

"Yes, pyramid. The pyramids of Egypt, one of the Seven Wonders of the world, so far, 5,000 years of history. It has many strange phenomena: put milk and meat in the tower, can be long-term preservation; joint pain, toothache, general fatigue, stayed in the tower for a while, you can reduce pain; Pharaoh remains in the tower calendar recurring 5,000 years is still preserved, pyramid thus called the 'magic tower', it can gather cosmic energy.

"The 52-degree angle, square pyramidal-shaped the bit synchronous movement with the magnetic field lines is the stability of the mysteries of the pyramids. The best posture should be a double disc, with the stature of this practice, the fastest get power, easily supernatural power, which is the practice of shape of the mysteries."

"Wow! I always thought oriental culture is very mysterious, it has such a deep scientific reason." Rosalyn smiled.

"That's why we come to learn."

"Yes, it's so interested."

Peter looked down there at the Huang Pu River cruise under the tower through floor-to-ceiling windows, he saw that there was a cruise ship in the fireworks.

"What is that?" He asked.

"Some people may rent the cruise ship for a wedding banquet or birthday party or some celebration."

"Chinese is so rich!"

Jin smiled and said: "Some ones pursuit of fame, wealth and enjoyment, some ones pursuit of inner peace, and people live in different ways."

Peter got five plates of food, all kinds of salad and a some bread, all kind of the meat, some vegetable and soup, dessert, fruit, then went to get ice cream with Rosalyn. But Suraj didn't eat too much. Jin looked at him and asked in soft voice: "Raj are you ok? Don't like the food?"

Suraj closed eyes, hold hard didn't go to kiss her, then he answered: "I'm fine angel, I miss your congee."

When Peter sat down again, he said: "I like that Chinese buffet restaurant Mandarin in Toronto. Have you been to there Jin?"

"No." Jin smiled.

Peter shook head, said: "You know what? Jin, if I was your husband, I would lock you in a room, no TV, no phone, no music, no books, every day only give you some meat, cooked very well, would you like to eat?"

Rosalyn and Suraj laughed, Rosalyn said: "That's great, don't need to work, but can eat meat every day. If to me,

I would not eat the meat only, but also ask you for drink, after eat and drink, I just sleep."

Peter and Suraj laughed again.

"Ok, let's listen to Jin."

Jin smiled and shook head, said: "I won't eat the meat, I will sit in meditation there. No music, I can sing songs; no books, I can write blood poetry on the wall：'Life is precious, love is higher value. If for freedom, meat and husband can both be gave up.'"

Three people laughed again. Peter Riccardo shook head.

After dinner, they boarded a cruise ship too.

Suraj sat by Medie on the cruise, asked her: "What did you guys eat?"

"Vegetable." Medie said, "and no spicy, no soda drink, no coffee, these things are no good for meditation. We try to eat alkaline foods to keep our blood clean."

"Wow, it seems I should learn more nutrition." Suraj nodded then asked again, "Medie, if would every body like to be vegetarian in your family?"

"No, from beginning, no. We had never force our child to do it, we tell them the reason, then let them make choice by themselves. The 5th girl Yu took two years to change, we cooked special for her every day."

Suraj nodded, he took a deep breath then asked: "Medie, may I ask, don't you and Jin intend to get married?"

Medie looked at Oriental Pearl tower, said: "Frankly, I don't believe in marriage, I don't believe there is still so much long-lasting love in the world, because I have seen too much betrayal and games. This is a era of lovers, rather than a era of love. People are getting more meretricious, pursuit of personal enjoyment, a man makes many girl friends at same time, have wine today, drunk today. Can You offer your heart, your body and your life into an unreliable person like this?"

Suraj silence, and his heart felt so heavy, because he knew that what Medie says was true. But he said: "Do you not believe there are some good men in the world?"

"Yes I do," Medie said, "but a good man does not mean that is a suitable man to me. Falling in love with a man is a misstep. I think, and marriage is the greater adventure, I'm afraid I afford to lose, I'm afraid of disappointment, so I will not go to hope."

Suraj sighed: "Medie, if anyone hurt you before?"

"No, thanks God! So it's not late to choose a better way. You know, I study Buddhist life science."

"Yah I know, you study and want nirvana. Well, how about Jin? Did she held the same views with you?"

"Jin is a universal lover, any time when she saw any body need help, she always will give a hand. She always drives at left line or center line, never block the cars witch turning right. She pursuits of inner peace and quiet, I don't know if there will be a man can go same way with her, I think it's hard. She has six children have to the take care and upbringing, she won't have time to have her own children, she hope that all the good men can get married and have their own child."

Suraj looked at Jin, she was sitting at other side with children. Children were not problem to Suraj to love Jin, even share life with her, the problem that stop him to love her was that secret in his heart.

"Were you and Jin born in the year of dragon?" Suraj asked Medie again.

"Yah."

"I am monkey, dragon and monkey are best relationship." Medie looked at Suraj surprised and laughed: "You even studied this! Wow! But, you know, we have six kids, we have to work hard to make and save money for them."

"Surely I know. You sisters are great persons. I feel sorry I am not rich."

Medie looked at him, shook head: "Raj we are talking about love, not money. Our kids had never felt sorry because Jin and me are not rich."

"You are right." Suraj nodded. "I got some students, I mean I teach piano after work, I try to make more money, so maybe one day, I can help your family."

Medie looked at Suraj: "Thank you Raj! We didn't know it. But please don't work too hard, you also need to take good care of yourself."

"I will. Thank you too!"

At this time, they heard of a double violin ensemble, they turned to look, that was actually Rosalyn and the 2nd girl Shang were playing, they both stood on the side of the ship, Peter was taking video for them. They attracted all tourists. When the end of the song, they won the applause of the full boat. Then, five girls sang two songs in cappella. The music was that melodious, sweet, sprinkling to the river.

"So beautiful—the songs, the sconce, and the singers." Suraj said.

Medie smiled and said: "Yes, they are." Then she told Suraj that Jin was making MTV, Jin said that she would use this DVD album to make the money back witch the all cost for this trip in China. This was a travel, and also a business.

Suraj shook his head again: "Jin's so smart, she's a genius. Who will not love her?!"

Next day, they visited EXPO, then went to Nan Jing Road for shopping. After dinner, they came to Waitan. Waitan was known as the top financial of China and the Oriental Wall Street.

Suraj and Jin walked alone the bound of Huang Pu River, enjoyed the beautiful night view.

"Jin, do you know? my grandfather had once lived in Shanghai." Suraj said, his sound was heavy.

"Oh? Had never heard you talked about. "Jin stopped, looked at him.

"He was a German Jew, a pianist, in order to escape Nazi persecution, he followed a friend to come to Shanghai, lived in the International refugee camps where he met my father, an Russian orphan, the boy playing the harmonica very well. Grandpa liked him, took care him and shelter him. Later grandpa fell in love with a Chinese nurse, she worked for the Red Cross. But soon, in an air strike, the girl covered my father with her body, she saved my father, then she died."

Suraj sighed: "After the war, grandpa took my father came to U.S.. My father married a Indian girl, but my mother got a accident then past away. 20 years ago, my grandpa and father returned to Europe, grandpa asked my father took him to Shanghai, After back home, sooner he past away."

Jin was reticent, then whispered: "God bless you Raj, your grandpa, your father, the Chinese girl, and all peace-loving people."

Suraj silently hold Jin in his arms, looking at the shimmering waves of the Huang Pu River, said: "I'd like to thank the city and its people."

Next day, they visited EXPO, then, every body said By to Shanghai.

3

"We are not going to Hong Kong this time." The 1st girl Gong said.

"It's too hot right now in Hong Kong!" The 5th girl Yu said.

After the colorful Shanghai, Beijing was also beautiful more than Suraj's imagine.

Their bus was running on Capital International Airport ExHyw, then came to Chang'an Avenue, they saw Tian An Men square, the biggest square in the world. When they turned to south of Rainbow Bridge from Fu Xing Men, Medic pointed a tall building on left side to Suraj Ram:

"That is the Central Conservatory of Music, Jin, pianist Lang Lang, Yun Di Li were all students here. Vanessa-Mae Nicholson (Chen) had also been here to learn violin from Professor Yaoji Lin, the College is now ranked to be the top ten music academy in the world."

Suraj nodded, at this moment, their bus had past Xi Bian Men, Medie pointed to the right side, an ancient city wall ruins, and said: "It is the old Ming Dynasty city walls of Beijing, has five hundred years already."

"Five hundred years? Oh!" Suraj exclaimed.

That night, Jin's family were together with their parents and three foreign guests had dinner at Quan Ju

De toast duck restaurant. But Jin's family was vegetarian, they didn't eat duck or any meat, they came here were only for friends. During the dinner, they also watched the performances, Beijing opera, magic, shadow play. People gave cheers and applaud again and again, kept to take video and pictures.

Jin booked Beijing International Hotel. located at the Chang An Ave. East. Rooms are large, modern facilities, furniture rather special. Whole window wall face to north, they could overlook the beautiful night view of Chang'an Avenue, Medie brought three friends going to the top floor of the hotel for dinner, that was a revolving buffet restaurant, three foreigners are very satisfied.

It was raining outside, Suraj could not sleep, he took a shower, then went to the bed, turned on the TV, then turned off, turned on lap top to go internet, then logged off, he turned over and over on the bed, he only thought about Jin. Jin and Medie took six kids lived in two twin rooms at next floor for saving money, they ordered folding beds. How come Jin didn't send Ark to be here, shared the room with him? She must hope him to get more relax. Suraj wanted to know what were they doing now, but he thought that maybe they were sleeping already, better don't interrupt.

Suraj sighed in the darkness, then got up, took some drink from the mini bar. At this time, he heard that there was a tiny sound at the door, his musician's ears are very sensitive. He listened again, no more sound, he walk to the door, then saw a business card was there on the floor, had just been filled in from the crack.

"What's that?" Suraj picked it up and took a look, it was unexpectedly a massage girl's card, a very young Chinese girl on the front of the card, the other side was a white girl with hot sexy clothing.

Suraj tore the card to be two pieces, threw into the garbage bin. At this moment, he notice that small basket on the table, there was a razor, a map in it, and also a condom.

"They offer this kind of thing?!" Suraj Ram felt surprised, "People said that Chinese is conservative and reserved, just like this? So open!"

Suraj came to the window. Raining was so heavy outside, made him miss Jin more, but he didn't know whether should court her, there was a secret in his heart, always fight to him, stop him to love Jin. Suraj felt painful so much. He had drunk done the wine mouthful, then, he decided to go swimming.

Suraj took elevator to downstairs fitness area, he walked the pool room and saw five girls actually were sitting in a row at the edge of the pool in meditation, Ark was swimming alone in the pool; then Suraj saw Rosalyn was in sauna and Peter in the gym room. Suraj almost laughed, it seemed that not him only could not sleep. But where was Jin? He didn't see Jin. Medie was responsible for taking care of the kids, she moved her lips to tell Suraj that Jin was in the lobby. Suraj thanked her, turned around and left.

He heard of a soft and familiar piano sound when he walked closed to the lobby rest area, that was "The Girl On The Balance Beam—Elf Of Night" he wrote. Suraj's heart got moved and warm up, the he saw Jin was sitting by the piano. It was 10:30 at night now, but there were still a few of listeners sitting in the sofa behind Jin. Suraj gently walked over to sit down. The music was beautiful, the player was beautiful. Suraj looked at Jin, really want to hold her to spend this beautiful night together and share this life. But what was Jin's willing? Suraj wanted to know the answer in every second.

The end of the song, applause sounded, a couple of foreign elderly left a tip on the piano before leaving, they even kissed Jin's forehead, said: "So beautiful, darling, have a good night!"

Jin thanked them, then continued to play. Suraj now gently came to sit down beside Jin, used left hand to take her accompaniment parts, Jin smiled and looked at him, they played together to finish Chopin's Nocturne.

"I didn't know you also have such a part time job." Suraj holed Jin's left hand, they left the piano.

When the door of the glass elevator opened at the top level, Suraj didn't move. They both looked at out side, it was still raining, and very heavy now, Chang'an Ave. was wet, tremble and beautiful. Suraj didn't want to leave, even one more second longer with Jin, he wanted to kiss and hug her in the rainy night, in the glass elevator, at the 28th floor, but he was not sure if it was the due time, right place and good form. Then he heard of Jin' soft voice:

"Raj, go back to sleep, our ancients Chinese called this two hours is 'Zi Shi' that is from 23:00 to 1:00, it means 'Rat Time', Yin is turning to yang, every body should go to sleep before this time, otherwise, your body would soon be getting old."

Suraj was listening, but still didn't move, then he asked: "What is Yin and yang? angel."

Jin looked at him, then she use her cell phone to show Suraj a photo, said: "This is Tai Chi, white is yang, black is yin. Yin includes yang, yang includes yin, without yang, no yin; without yin, no yang. Ying and yang can exchange. Sun is Yang, moon is yin; day time is yang, night time is yin; summer is yang, winter is yin; man is yang, woman is yin; fire is yang, water is yin; palm is yang, the back of your hand is yin. Right now, yin is changing to be yang, at 6 o'clock in the morning, yin and yang is balance; when the time is at 12 o' clock at noon, yang changes to be yin; at 6 o'clock at dusk, yang and yin is balance. If you got sick, that means yin and yang in your body lost balance. Right now, if you didn't go to sleep . . . ."

"If I went to sleep before 'Zi Shi' every night, I would not see you on that balance beam in that stormy night, last year."

Jin looked at him. Suraj also looked at Jin's eyes, whispered: "I had been wanting to ask you, angel, why did you go to walk on that balance beam in that stormy night? What was happened in your life at that time? Would you mind to tell me?"

Jin looked at him, then said: "I got too much pressures in my life, it was so hard to us in Canada from beginning, I almost fell down at that time. I was trying to control and balance myself, to be stronger. I pray every day, say: God,

I need a orchestra and a chorus. Thanks God we met you. I had been thinking you are an angel God sent to us."

Suraj smiled: "I saw. But, you had a very good job in China before, how come, you and Medie just gave up every thing, brought six kids to be Canada?"

"For the education of our kids." Jin said.

Suraj nodded: "You paid too much for them."

"And I got so much too." Jin smiled.

"Yah, it's more blessed to give than to receive. You are so nice, angel. We are so lucky to have you."

"Thank you my friend, I am lucky to have you too."

Suraj liberalized Jin's left hand, but hugged the right shoulder of her, then said: "Do you think, If no woman, man would lose the balance of yin-yang?"

Jin didn't answer, she thought for a moment, then said: "You know what, Raj, that balance beam is my ark, that ark is my shore, that shore is my heart, that dark night is the boundless sea, I have been on shore, do not want to be ups and downs again."

Suraj felt confused, he didn't understand what Jin was taking about.

Jin then turned on her cell phone, to show Suraj a photo. Suraj took a look, that was four Chinese characters" 回头是岸".

"What does this mean angel?" Suraj asked.

"I'd like to leave this question to you, Raj, What's this words mean? through this trip, you will find out the answer, then tell me later. Don't ask any body, don't search it on Internet before you fine out it. I will send it to your cell phone later."

"Ok, angel."

"Well, better go to sleep now." Jin looked at him.

Suraj gently hugged Jin in to his affectionate embrace, he closed eyes, then he heard thunder outside, the rain was more heavy now. He hug Jin tight, one second, two seconds, he wanted longer, but Jin gently patted his back.

Suraj kissed her forehead, then let her go.

"Good night! Raj. Sweet dreams." Jin smiled, then got out the glass elevator.

"Good night! angel." Suraj still stood there until the elevator took him away.

Next morning, after breakfast in hotel, Medie said that she would take them three friends going to Wang Fu Jing Shopping Mall buying cell phones.

Suraj asked her immediately: "Where is Jin going to?"

Medie said: "She will take kids to a publish house in the morning, their book 《Love—The Best Gift》 got published."

"Wow! Really!" Three friends felt so happy for them.

"Congratulations!" Peter Riccardo said.

"Jin is a great teacher and mother!" Rossalyn said.

"Yes, she is! We're so proud of her!" Medie said.

"And we are looking forward to the English edition of the book." Suraj said.

"They are doing now, it's coming soon." Medie.

"Great! I love it!"

The shops and folk sculpture on the both side of the commercial pedestrian street were very attractive. So many shoppers came from different places, different countries. Rosalyn wanted to try different snacks. Peter took lots of pictures.

Suraj sent the first text message to Jin as soon as he got new phone.

"I want to c u all the time, angel!"

In a supermarket, Suraj saw a lot of flavor food that he had never ate before, and all of them looked delicious too, he and his friends push a shopping cart with Medie, walk around. Riccard and Rosalyn were looking for what they want to try, just like a mouse fell into rice tank, but Suraj felt that he wanted nothing.

"You look tired man." Riccard pet him on the shoulder.

Be careful don't get sick Raj, we are in travel now." said Rosalyn.

"I know. Thanks! Don't worry." Suraj sighed.

"Raj, do you know what is my favorite dessert?" Medie looked at him, smiled and asked.

"Saqi Ma." Suraj remembered that Medie told him when once they shopped at T & T Supermarket in Toronto, all of Chinese supermarkets in Toronto sold Saqi Ma, and many flavors, but Medie didn't like them, Jin said that Medie only liked Dao Xiang Cun's Saqi Ma in Beijing. Suraj then thought. what was different the Dao Xiang Cun's Saqi Ma in Beijing?

Now Medie had finally came back to Beijing after four-years' expectations. She walked to the dessert section, asked a young girl seller for couple of pounds Dao Xiang Cun's Saqi Ma. She talked to the young girl when she got her Saqi Ma, said:

"You don't know how lucky you are to work here, young sister, every day you sell Saqi Ma, I have dreamed of our Beijing's Saqi Ma in a another country for four years. Many times I dreamed to be here to buy Saqi Ma, bought a big box, but not go home to eat yet, just woke up."

Suraj nodded. Rosalyn said that she could understand, hometown's food made people miss hometown.

Riccardo couple also bought two packs of Beijing flavor food, they feel so happy. Suraj then asked how come Chinese have so many snacks, looked almost thousands kinds, makes him dazzling.

"Five thousand years food culture, what do you think!" Rossalyn says with a smile.

Back to the hotel, everybody washed hands, then open the plastic bag on the table, Medie installed Saqi Ma in paper plates.

"Let's try now!" She says.

"Yah, let's try what's special of Beijing's Saqi Ma?" Suraj sit on the sofa, he bite a little bit, soft sweet taste immediately makes him exclaimed:

"So Good!"

"Yah, it's really delicious!" Peter and Rosalyn also repeatedly praised.

But Suraj saw tears was coming out from Medie's eyes when she ate the first piece.

4

Before they came to Beijing, Jin had booked tickets of two concerts online. Medie told Suraj, when they lived in Beijing before, on weekend, they often took children to see a concert, but since they went to Canada, they don't have money to concert any more.

The first concert was at National Center for Performing Arts where was beside Tian An Men Square, the young Chinese violinist Dan Zhu cooperated with the National Ballet Orchestra and a German conductor, played Brahms's Violin Concerto in D major and his No.2 Symphony in D major, etc.

When they sat in the auditorium, Medie told Suraj, the Philharmonic Orchestra who performed tonight was just the one Jin had worked for before, and the songs tonight, all were from Jin's favorite German composer Brahms. Medie had been to Europe to show when she went to university and as a member of China National Symphony Orchestra Children and Young Woman Choir, took that opportunity she went to Hamburg, Germany, Jin was studying there in Berlin, they were together to go to the former residence of Brahms memorial. Medie still remembered, they took subway first came to St. Pauli, and after another 10 minutes of walking, in a very secluded little street called Peterstrasse, they saw an ancient house. Medie took out a plastic card to show Suraj, it was a light blue face value of 100 German Mark bill, the front was Clark. Schumann's photos, at the back was the piano she used. Brahms loved her in his whole life.

After that performance, everyone took pictures with the beautiful building-National Center for performing and Arts, the building was also Jin's favorite mode of construction—arc-type, all-glass shell, on the water; it constantly, gracefully changes with Jin's favorite colors—purple, blue and white.

Riccardo couple had been taking video, while constantly praise, said: "So beautiful! when can we come here to perform?"

Jin and Medie took children and three friends to visit historical sites in Beijing—Temple of Heaven, Forbidden City, Summer Palace, Bird's Nest National

Stadium, Olympic Center, also toured around the capital city, and shopping at Silk Street, Oriental Plaza and City Philharmonic.

5

The next day, sky was clear, they rented a small bus, went to Ba Da Ling Great Wall, Jin drove. Before departure, Jin and Medie specifically went to their mother's home, got some long hook, clip, and many big plastic bags. Suraj asked them what's these staff for? Jin said:

"You will know when we get the Great Wall."

Now it was not the best season to the Great Wall, but still a lots of tourists. People took cable car up to the mountain, then Suraj proposed that everybody competed to climb to the beacon "Hero Slope", that was the top of Ba Da Ling Great Wall, and also the highest peak of the Great

Wall. Eleven people just started, the result was, Suraj and Ark were champions. Children were very excited, they took photos and videos together, everyone was standing on the beacon, looked around mountains, could see very far.

Jin asked Suraj: "Do you know how long is the Great Wall?"

"Very long," Suraj said, "as long as how far from Canada to China, as long as how far is from you to me."

Jin smiled, then said: "It's over six thousand seven hundred kilometers long." She took out a tourist guide of the Great Wall, pointed the picture to show Sauraj:

"The Great Wall of Jia Yu Guan is the western end of the Great Wall, the city grand advantageous, both sides of the city across the Gobi Desert, is the throat of traffic to Hexi Corridor, the pearl on the ancient Silk Road. The city's design compact, construction strict, according to legend when material is also very accurate account of labor, after the completion, remaining only one brick, was placed on the upstairs in the building as a souvenir, it was in the year 1372."

"Great!" Suraj praised.

Jin was overlooking the distant then continues: "When the 5th girl Yu was 1 year old, still could not walk, Medie and me decided to take her here on her birthday. I still remember that day in fall, the mountains was green, yellow and red, the sky was very blue. We hold Yu, came up to the Beacon "Hero Slope" here, then we put down her, I took off her shoes, let the kid stood there by herself leaning on the wall. Yu had never walked independently, only in our hands, or used the walker to help, two legs always shook. But that day she was very excited, staring curious eyes, looked around at people and blue sky, overlooking the picturesque mountains and the Great Wall goes alone from her feet to far away, she stood very straight, one hand leaning on the wall, another hand waved, looked like a true man of indomitable spirit of the Great Wall. Medie took pictures for Yu, I was squatting a few paces far waving hand to the kid. So broad field, so excited, Yu seemed to jump, but sat down on the ground. Medie immediately wanted to hold Yu, I stopped her, we encourage Yu, Yu finally re-stood up by herself, then she enjoyed the good view again. Then, we called her name, shook her small shoes. Yu looked at us, laughing, then just moved her legs, one step, two steps, three steps, four steps . . . . She finally came into my arms. We were so pleased to hug her, she succeeded!"

Suraj looked at Jin with smile when she was taking, he always enjoyed to listen to her voice Jin said again: "The Great Wall goes through desert, mountains, until the head into the sea, can be said to symbolize life and concentrate the whole process. let the kid stand on the earth, climb on high mountains to overlook, his feet and his heart at the same time to experience thousands of years and learn the spirit from the Great Wall of Heaven, Earth, hum been. I hope that when Ark grows up, can has the open-mindedness likes the Great Wall across time and space, can has the soul likes the Great Wall lie thousands of miles, can has the tough and focused likes the Great Wall, has the faithful temperament like the great wall to change war to be peace. Jin said: Some kids learn walking on the bed, some ones start walking in flowers on the grass, some one in parents hands, today we take Ark climbing the Great Wall, not only to help him growth of his body but also and a leap of his spirit."

Suraj nodded head after hearing, and said: "To everybody who comes to the Great Wall, the mind will experience a leap." Then he put on headphones, start listening to the symphonic choral "The Great Wall" which composed by Jin, but he felt different this time to listen to this song with previous, he feels the mountains and the Great Wall in front of him, even the sky and everything seems to also chorus.

At this time, Medie led children play long sword on the beacon.

"Great music!" Suraj said in amazement, "great wall, great culture, great Chinese people."

Then, Jin lead every body came to the top of the beacon, Suraj played keyboard, Rosalyn and the 2nd girl Shang played violin, girls sang songs, Peter took video for them. Then Jin played Chinese Gu Qin, the 3rd girl Jiao played bamboo flute, others played Tai Chi sword in the music, Suraj played with them together. Many tourist stood around to watch them, gave them hot applause.

Suraj felt so good, it was wonderful experience to him, he could play music and Tai Chi on the Great Wall, he gave Jin a big hug, said: "Thank you so much! Angel."

But the following program was a surprise to Suraj Ram—to be a volunteer, picking up garbage.

Everybody took a long-handled hook or clip, another hand takes a garbage bag, pick up plastic bottles, tin cans, foam lunch boxes or plastic bags, one by one put into garbage bags.

Medie told Suraj: "Before we went to Canada, in every fall, Jin and me took children to be here to pick up garbage as volunteers. We do not understand why people come here to throw garbage, such a so beautiful place, people had little respect for cultural heritage. We think that the major obstacle to environmental protection in China is a low level of education."

Half an hour later, they carried several bags of garbage, walked down to the mountain, then put into big garbage bin.In a souvenir shop, three foreign friends bought some T-shirts of the Great Wall, and post cards, fans and tea cups.

6

About the second concert in Beijing, Jin and Medie did not tell anything to three friends. When they came to Beijing Concert Hall after dinner, Suraj asked what the show was tonight? Jin smiled and said: "Deep breath, you will know later even if I didn't tell you."

They sat in left side seats of the VIP row. Jin said that it was her favorite position, she often sat here before, if there was no more ticket for here, she would sit upstairs on the left wing where she can see the piano on the stage, Medie and the children now were sitting there.

Suraj saw a lot of audience tonight, there were many children.

"Jin?" Jin heard of someone was calling her name. Then she stood up, shook hands with a 40 years old Chinese lady, they both stand there talking, Jin turned to Suraj, Peter and Rosalyn, introduces them said: "My friends from Canada.

The lady said Hi in English, she had seen their performances in Los Angeles, she was their audience and very happy to meet them here.

After the lady left, a foreign couple walked into the VIP seats. When they were pass in front of Jin, the lady stopped, she looked at Jin, and then asked her in Chinese: "Excuse me, are you . . . . Jin Qin?"

Jin looked at the 50-year-old lady, stood up and answered in English.

The lady smiled: "Yes, I had seen your choir performances in German embassy about six or seven years ago."

Jin suddenly realized, shook hands with her and said in German: "Nice to meet you again! You have a splendid memory!"

"So, where is Medie?" The lady asked.

"She is upstairs there with children." Jin replied.

"Oh, please say Hi to them for me."

"Thank you! I will."

Jin sat down when the lady past. Suraj asked her: "Your audience again?"

Jin nodded and said: "Yah, she is the German Embassy Diplomat, and her husband is Cultural Counselor of German embassy. They often hold a small concert on weekend, we went to performances there before many times."

"So long, she still can remember you!"

Jin smiled: "I think this may be the diplomatic talent. In addition, When Medie and I are together, always gave people some impression."

"That's true, you sisters look like each other too much." Suraj smiled.

The show finally started, not as Suraj's imagine, there were neither chairs on the stage nor a scores shelves, only a piano there. Then, Suraj saw four teams of boys and girls dressed in school uniforms from both sides onto the stage, audience gave applause. Then, a 70-year old conductor and a lady who was wearing a white dress took the stage. Audience applause on the issue even more.

Now Suraj realized that this was indeed a surprise that Jin gave to him. During the show, Jin's eyes were tears. The familiar melody and scenarios touch her a lot. Jin felt thanks so much to the chorus' founder and conductor—Professor Hong Nian Yang, in 20 years, he worked hard to make this excellent chorus to be world-class, Children And Young Women Chorus Of The China National Symphony Orchestra made so many children's dreams grow wings, music affect their lives, even their children.

Jin once said: Every country, city, district and school should have their chorus, children chorus, youth chorus, adult chorus, senior chorus. Choral Arts is very harmonious and beautiful, able to unite the hearts of people together.

After the show, Suraj follows Jin and Medie come to the backstage to visit Yang Hongnian and his wife—pianist and artistic director Professor Tang Chong Qing, bouquets of flowers. Two teachers saw them, so happy to give them a big hug, Professor Yang kindly asked about their life and work in Canada, he saw their show in Los Angeles on TV, it was great, he felt so proud of them.

Suraj took pictures and video of Jin sisters and their two teachers, some of the choir kids recognized that they all ran to take pictures with Jin sisters. Professor Yang looked at these kids, smiled and felt so happy.

7

Came to Beijing one week, they left this city, eleven people start the trip again.

From the natural landscape to the cultural landscape, literature, art, architecture, technology, religion, food, and even a ghost culture. Jin made the plan for the whole tour routes and attractions, booked the hotels and restaurants where the most distinctive.

The 1st day: from Beijing to Xi'an in the morning.

On the airplane, Jin told their three friends: Shaanxi Province is one of civilized important, all together China headstream, as far back as having Lantian Man to grow work here right away in the front for 1000000 years, starting from the 11th century B.C., successively have 13 in history dynasty found a capital here. Shaanxi Province field of being that Chinese cultural relics and historic sites gathers together, name of having "the natural history museum "Shaanxi is not only a lot of cultural relics and historic, but also natural scene is beautiful. Xi'an City and Rome Italy, Greece Athens and Cairo Egypt are four famous ancient capital of the world's greatest civilizations, has been 1400 years of history, it was the capital city of 13 dynasties, including the most glorious Han Dynasty and Tang Dynasty. Xi'an has the world's best preserved ancient city wall and many historical relics. In 1998, when Bill Clinton became U.S. president, the first country his official visiting was China, but the first city he came to in China was not Beijing, not Shanghai, not Hong Kong, but Xi'an. When President Clinton arrived in Xi'an, Xi'an people welcome him in an ancient way they put down the drawbridge gate, covered with red carpet, let the president and first lady to walk into the city Xi'an, came up to the city wall. President Clinton said in the speech: "We respect and surprise the miracle and culture of Chinese people created here. I have been longing for here when I grew up, it's finally today, the dream come true." The next day, President Clinton, his wife and daughter visited the Terracotta Warriors.

Then, Jin showed them the DVDs of Zhang Yi Mou and Jackie Chan's movies which were about the Terracotta Warriors.

Lunch: Tong Sheng Xiang Restaurant. It was a very famous flavor restaurant in Xi'an.

Afternoon: Go to Xi'an City Wall.

In Ming Dynasty started building the wall in the year 1370, so it's about 800 years old; it's one of the oldest and best preserved Chinese city walls, it's one of the most important things in Xi'an, to visit the City Wall, definitely, because it's something typical. You can take a look at Bell Tower and Drum Tower, you can look outside of the city. If the weather is nice and you are lucky, you can see the mountains around Xi'an. The Xi'an City Wall is one of the most beautiful landmarks in Xi'an, it's something typical. Going up on the City Wall, you have a beautiful view of the Bell Tower, the Drum Tower, the ancient center of the city as well as the rest of Xi'an. It's definitely worth visiting. Going around the walls, you can see every neighborhood and just the diversity, everybody is so different and the way they live is so visible. It's one of the great things about Xi'an.

Every body rented a bike, Riccardo and Rosalyn even rented a tandem bike any side of the wall and ride it around, it's about a 13 kilometers tiring, but it's a great way to see the city.

After that, eleven people come to Dayan Pagoda.

Dayan Pagoda has seven stories and is 64.5 meters high, it is situated in the great Ci'en Temple to the south of the city of Xi'an.

Jin explained in English to three friends said:

"Dayan Tower was originally built in 652 during the reign of Emperor Gao Zong of the Tang Dynasty (618-907), it functioned to collect Buddhist materials that were taken from India by the hierarch Xuan Zang. Xuan Zang started off from Chang'an (the ancient Xi'an), along the Silk Road and through deserts, finally arriving in India, the cradle of Buddhism. Enduring 17 years and traversing 100 countries, he obtained Buddha figures, 657 kinds of sutras, and several Buddha relics. Having gotten the permission of Emperor Gao Zang (628-683), Xuan Zang, as the first abbot of Da Ci'en Temple, supervised the building of a pagoda inside it. With the support of royalty, he asked 50 hierarchs into the temple to translate Sanskrit in sutras into Chinese, totaling 1,335 volumes, which heralded a new era in the history of translation. Based on the journey to India, he also wrote a book entitled 'Pilgrimage to the West' in the Tang Dynasty, to which scholars attached great importance. Had you heard about this words: 'Saving a life exceeds building a seven-storied pagoda.'? no? ok, but every body knows the story of Monkey King protect Monk Xuan Zang to India right?"

At dusk, they sat with many tourists beside the Dayan Pagoda North square, to enjoy Asia's largest musical fountain lights show.

Dinner: De Chang Fa dumpling Restaurant.

Three foreign friends felt very excited, it was their first time to eat dumplings, and they had to use chopsticks. Jin ordered a special combo for them—one hundred kinds of shapes and flavors dumplings, colorful, cooked in different way, boil, steam, pan fried, soup, hot pot, and some dumplings are smaller than your nail, some dumplings look like chicken, rabbit, swan, very cute, as well as side dishes and dessert. Every body relished the food. They again and again to take pictures. After dinner, they watched a show of Tang Dynasty dance.

Rosalyn said: "This tour is so fantastic! Jin thank you so much! You are a wonderful tour guide."

Suraj thought that was really hard to be a vegetarian when he saw Jin and children were sitting at another table to eat vegetarian dumplings, he felt sad, he wanted to move to be there with them, but his efforts failed.

8

The 2nd day: They rented a bus from Xi'an International Travel Service to Huaqing Pool. The Huaqing Pool was located in the Lintong District 30 km east to the urban area of Xi'an, on the north side of Lishan Mount. It boasted the natural hot springs. The favorable geographical condition and natural environment make it one of the cradles where ancient people settled. It was also a favorite place for emperors to build their palaces as a resort. Since ancient times, it has ever been a famous bathing and tourist destination.

According to historical recorded and archeological the Huaqing Pool had a history of 6000 years for the use of hot springs and a history of 3000 years of royal gardens.

This was the first time they used the hot spring to wash hands and face.

The next stop was the tomb of Qin Shi Huang, it was near an earthen pyramid 76 meters tall and nearly 350 meters square. The tomb presently remained unopened. There were plans to seal-off the area around the tomb with a special tent-type structure to prevent corrosion from exposure to outside air. However, there was at present only one company in the world that makes these tents, and their largest model will not cover the site as needed.

Qin Shi Huang's necropolis complex was constructed to serve as an imperial compound or palace. It was comprised of several offices, halls and other structures and was surrounded by a wall with gateway entrances. The remains of the craftsmen was working in the tomb may also be found within its confines, as it was believed that they were sealed inside alive to keep them from divulging any secrets about its riches or entrance. It was only fitting, therefore, to have this compound protected by the massive terra cotta army interred nearby.

Then they went to Terra Cotta Warriors Museum.

The Terracotta Warriors and Horses were a collection of 8,099 life-size terra cotta figures of warriors and horses located in the Mausoleum of the First Qin Emperor. The figures were discovered in 1974 near Xi'an, Shaanxi province. The terracotta figures were buried with the first Emperor of Qin (Qin Shi Huang) in 210-209 BC. Consequently, they were also sometimes referred to as "Qin's Army."

The Terracotta Army of China was discovered in March 1974 by local farmers drilling a well to the east of Mount Li. Mount Li was the name of the man-made necropolis and tomb of the First Emperor of Qin; Qin Shi Huang.

Construction of this mausoleum began in 246 B.C. and was believed to had taken 700,000 workers and craftsmen in 36 years to complete. Qin Shi Huang was interred inside the tomb complex upon his death in 210 B.C. According to the Grand Historian Sima Qian, The First Emperor was buried alongside great amounts of treasure and objects of craftsmanship, as well as a scale replica of the universe complete with gemmed ceilings representing the cosmos, and flowing mercury, representing the great earthly bodies of water. Recent scientific worked at the site had shown high levels of mercury in the soil of Mount Li, tentatively indicating an accurate description of the site's contents by Sima Qian.

At last, they saw the museum's honorary curator Zhi Fa Yang, an ordinary peasant, in 1974, he discovered the world's eighth wonder when he was drilling a well, but now, he was a man who shook hands and took pictures with the most heads of countries in the world, if it was not because President Clinton wanted to meet him and also asked him to sign, until now, he would still didn't know even one Chinese character, he had never been to school.

Three foreign friends heard of this, immediately went to buy a English book witch was about terracotta warriors and horses, and took it to ask Mr. Yang sign for them.

Dinner: Lao Sun foam bun. It's also the famous flavor in Xi'an.

The 3rd Day: Huashan Mountain tour.

Huashan was the root of Chinese culture, many Chinese name "Hua" would be from here.

Mt. Huashan was about 120 kilometers (about 75 miles) east of Xi'an City in Shaanxi Province. Huashan was one of the five sacred mountains of China, its five main peaks shaped much like a flower. Huashan was historically the location of several influential Taoist monasteries, and was known as a center for the practice of traditional Chinese martial arts. This mountain was celebrated for its majestic breath-taking crags, steep paths, beautiful scenery and it was said to be the most precipitous mountain in the world. Until recently there was only one way to reach the top of Mt. Huashan since ancient times. Most of the trail was very narrow and steep; some parts were almost vertical. Iron chains had been set up along the path, but courage and an adventurous spirit were still necessary if you decide to climb Mt. Huashan on foot. Recent developments had added two alternate ways of traveling to the summit. Now people could take the ropeway, or rode in a cable car to enjoy the unique scenery of Mt. Huashan.

Took cable car, through the clouds, then they began climbing the mountain, to many of them, his was the first time. “I have never witnessed such a high, so steep and so beautiful mountain.” Rosalyn said.

Jin reminded everyone: “The Mountain road is very precipitous, every body must be careful, stay together, safety first.”

Huashan ancient road, its dangerous to make everyone be tightly together, help each other, encouraged each other. Children were very strong, they always gave people hands. At the Ladder Dragon, every body had to clutch tunic ides climbing, all seemed ape. Suraj sweat a lot, he saw several over 60-year-old Chinese people were also climbing, he gasped, and shook head.

“Don’t keep to rush,” Jin told every one, “Ancient Chinese said: stop, then you could watch. We come to conquer Huashan, but also to enjoy the scenery. We effort on the road of life, but also need to enjoy life.”

When they felt too tired, just sat down beside the road to have a rest, but no body gave up. At every stop, they saw different view.

Along the way, they past Yuquan Palace, a famous Quanzhen sect of Taoism Palace in Mt. Huashan. Then they saw a priests lied on the top of wall beside the road, only one brick wide, and other side was bottomless deep valleys. It shocked Rosalyn and Peter a lot. Jin, but made Suraj thought the scene that Jin walked on the balance beam in that stormy night. He knew that people could control their own body and mind, and to achieve this concentration.

When they reached Sky Plank of Nan Tian Men, everyone put up their own peace lock or concentric lock on the iron chains, then thrown the key into the valley.

Took six hours, finally they boarded onto the top of the peak, they felt that sky was so close and they could touch the stars in the sky. South peak elevation of 2160.5 meters, it was the highest main peak of Huashan. Full of fresh air, every one took a deep breath. Everywhere they look around, saw beautiful panoramic view, rolling hills, the Yellow River such as silk, such as cotton, every body really appreciate Huashan steep majestic broad momentum, enjoyed impressive heaven, Jin then told every body, Huashan was thousands feet high, at its peak there was a small pool concave three feet, shine upon light of day. Poet Du Fu called it "True Source." The more the great metaphor, the more open-minded, humble.

Then, girls sang Jin's 《Chinese fantasy symphonic choral—Mt. Huashan》 in cappella harmony, every tourist stopped to watch them, and gave them hot applause.

When three foreign friends sat down to relax, Jin lead children to play Tai Chi sword, then, they sat down on the big rock, faced to distance, stayed in meditation.

Medie said to three friends that it was a wonderful place here for meditation, on the so high and quiet mountain, over the cloud, the sky was so broad, and the air was so clean.

Three friends closed legs, hands and eyes, learned and experienced meditation too. Suraj sat by Jin, but only ten seconds, he just opened one eye, he worried about their bags.

"Your body has sat down, but your heart has not yet." He heard a voice said.

Dinner: Xi'an Restaurant, one of the most famous flavor restaurants in Xi'an.

Everyone ordered their most favorite food. Suraj asked Jin if they had Tofu Seaweed Seafood Soup on the Manu.

Jin said: "Sorry there is no this soup here, and this soup will hurt your stomach, because it is cool."

Suraj, Rosalyn and Peter puzzled, it was obviously hot soup, how come Jin said that was cool?

Jin explained: "I said it's cool, doesn't mean the temperature, but the nature o of the food. For example, chili is put into refrigerator, when you take it out to eat, it's still spicy, make you hot, sweat, this is the nature of chili, because its molecules are very active, irritating to the human body, it can speed up blood circulation, make you sweat. Some foods, their molecules will absorb or take away our body's heat and make our blood cool. In Traditional Chinese Medicine said that this kind of food is called cold foods. TCM divided food and Chinese medicine into five nature—hot, such as: pepper, cinnamon; warm, such as: beef, lamb, chicken, onions, black tea, leeches; peaceful food, such as: grape, pineapple, rice, corn, pork, many kinds of fish and beans; cool, such as: wheat, green beans, duck, bananas, tomatoes, mushrooms, tofu; cold, such as: crabs, watermelon, bitter gourd, seaweed . . . . Hot and warm food is yang, cool and cold food is yin. Raj wanted seaweed tofu soup for dinner, to his cold and weak stomach, that's not a good idea."

The three foreign friends heard of these, felt very surprised. Rosalyn said: "I have lived four years old already, this is the first time to heard the food have different nature and yin-yang. The original food culture for thousands of years in China is really great."

Jin smiled and ordered a famous flavor in Xi'an—Pita Bread Soaked in Lamb Soup.

9

The 4th Day: Famen Tample

Famen Temple was located 110 kilometers east of Xi'an. Jin wanted to take her family and friends going to be there because Famen Temple enshrines Sakyamuni Buddha's phalanges relic(It's also called shrine), has lasted two thousand five hundred years, its existence was a miracle, to prove Buddhism was boundless, the compassion of Buddha was immeasurable. Whether it was no longer news in the more than a thousand years, or the brilliant and surprises in twenty years ago came back to light, in cosmic time, it was only a moment, but it symbolized the eternal of the Buddhist world.

Buddhist legend, when Buddha Sakyamuni Nirvana, the body health Sanmeizhenhuo, burning the body of immeasurable accumulation of merit, after seven days, leaving eight-four thousands crystal solid relic, leaving people to worship, planted enlightenment karma. Two hundred years later, to dominate the ancient Indus Valley in India Ashoka Peacock promote Buddhism asked the monks All Things Chorus put relic into eighty-four thousands contained, distributed to all over the world.

In 1987, Famen Temple rediscovered masterpieces of the Buddha's phalanges relic, the news was immediately shock the world Buddhist community. The history in eleven hundred years of history books, liked a miracle show out suddenly now, archaeologists were stunned, the masters, Buddhists were even more excited almost cried out. Famen Temple was re-expanded in large-scale, and held a grand esteeming ceremony for Buddha's finger bone. Since then, the Buddha's finger relic had been sent to Thailand, Hong Kong, Taiwan, South Korea, showing for broad public ceremony believers. In Thailand, the Thai prime minister, deputy prime minister and senior military representatives and the public, even King of Thai, Crown Prince and the monks went to worship. In Taiwan, the Famen Buddha's finger bone relic attracted a total of 800 thousands disciples went to worship. Buddha's finger relic came from north to the south of Taiwan to seat safety in Fo Guang Shan Temple, the believers up to 20 million kneeled along the road before the date. In 11 days, more than 2,000 groups and a million monks came to Fo Guang Shan to worship. Outside the building where Buddha's relic was, people were waiting on line one kilometers every day. Fo Guang Shan organized four ceremonies, to prove for over the thousand believers converted to Buddhism, the scene solemn and grand.

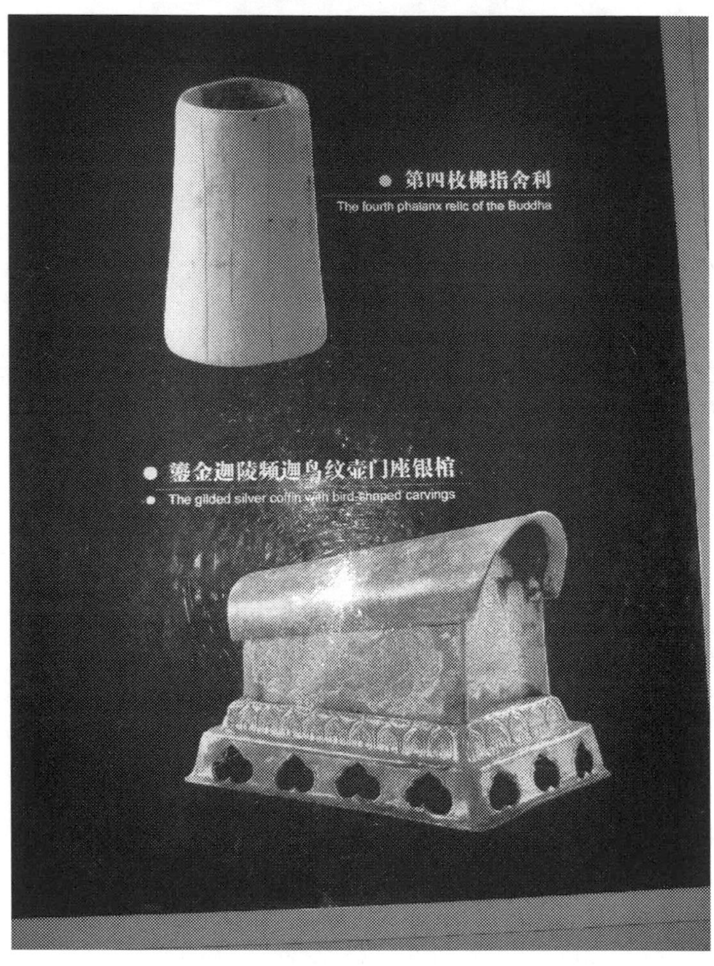

On the way, three friends asked Medie that how was relics formed.

Medie said: "If a Buddhist practitioner keep in meditation, vegetarian, no sex, no drink, no smoke, keeps inner-peace, later, will be full of essence in the body, when he past away, it's called 'Wang Sheng' in Buddhist, after the body was burned, would get some relic. Relics are some crystalline, very hard, even some soft tissue of body such as hair, muscle, tongue, brain and heart are able to form relics, in Buddhism, relics are holy in Buddhist."

"But how come some body like to live and dead in this way?" Peter Riccardo asked, "just think about it—no sex, no alcohol, no smoke, no meat, even no spicy food, no enjoy, what taste it is for the life?!"

"But all of these only can pleasure your body, some times, too many desires will bring trouble to you hurt you or some one else, lost balance, hat's why some people put down their desire, go to seek and keep peace and quiet for their physical and mental. This almost is the goal of all religions."

Every body nodded: "Get it."

10

The 5th day: They left the ancient city Xi'an in the morning, fly to city Chengdu.

Suraj didn't know why that every time when they took airplane, it was always Medie sat by him, Jin had never, he wanted to ask, but only shook head. After the airplane took off, Medie asked Suraj:

"Do you like Xi'an?"

"Sure, I do. You? have you been here before?"

"No, it's my first time."

"Really?! Just like me?!"

Medie smiled: "The traffic in this city is congested, some vehicles don't turn on the signals when they change lane, some ones got a little bit room just cut in, some ones make way to vied road, looks confused,."

"That's true," Suraj agreed, "because too many people here, every body needs the room."

"You are right. Also the public washroom, no matter the facilities is good or poor, people can not take breath, it really smelled bad!"

"That's why Jin gave every body the mask."

"She had the experience."

Only two hours for the flight, Suraj saw Ark and his five sisters were using tablets to read.

"What are they reading?" Suraj asked Medie.

"Gong is reading <<Feng Shui Architecture Design>>;" said Medie, "Shang is reading Joel Osteen's <<Become a Better You>>; Jiao is reading a Chinese novel, she said the writer Mo Yan would get Nobel Literature Prize; Zhi is reading Richard Dawkins' <<The God Delusion>>; Yu is reading Anne Lynn's novels <<Sublimation>> and <<Meditations In The Varicolored World>>; Ark, he is reading <<Mentality Curriculum Of Harvard>>."

"So good! These kids." Suraj then turned to look at Jin. Jin was sitting alone on the rear seat in meditation. It was Suraj first time to see somebody sit in meditation on airplane. He remembered the first time he saw a lady walking on the balance beam in the stormy night.

"Where is she now?"

"Let me show you" said Medie. She showed Suraj an image from her laptop, "This is Jin's ECG and EEG when she in the meditation state. Her heartbeat is very weak and slow, almost close to a straight line, but it runs extremely smooth, only a slight oscillation."

"God, this looks like the heartbeat of a dying person." Suraj said.

"In the meditation state, she almost does not burn calories, the essence of her body being crystal in gasified state, that is the production process of relic." Medie said.

Suraj shook his head: "She forgot all of us right now?"

"She has put everything down now."

Suraj looked back at Jin, suddenly he coughed hard twice, people who sat around him turned to look at him, but Jin did not moved. Suraj sighed, shook head and said, "Her heart is just like a piece of stone now."

Meide smiled: "She didn't forget us, she is just taking a short break, she's tired. Next stop, she would take better care of us."

Suraj nodded his head, and shook, then he put his sight out of window, he wanted to see every thing in the journey, even didn't want to wink.

Chengdu, capital city of Sichuan Province, one of the historical and cultural famous city in China, an important transportation hub in southwest China, five dynasties, over 2300 years of history, beautiful landscape, rich resources, the Three Kingdoms story every body can tell, Chan Tea, Chan silk and Chuan flavor is world-renowned.

After check in Chengdu Shangri-La Hotel, Jin rented a small bus, brought her tour group to visit Du Fu Thatched Cottage and the Temple of Marquis Wu. Du Fu was a famous poet in Tang Destiny, Marquis Wu means Zhuge Liang, one of the most smartest men in Chinese history, Jin had asked three foreign friends watching the movie DVD "Red Cliff" last night, the story talked about Zhu Ge Liang.

Then, Jin took the group to a tea house where was by a beautiful small lake, people came here drank tea, ate nuts, talked, read newspaper, played chess, watched show, you even could ask some body massaged for your shoulders, made you more relax.

"Oh, it's so good here!" Peter Riccardo said when he sat in the bamboo chair and enjoy the flower tea.

They talked about Chinese Tea Culture. Rosalyn said that her father was a tea lover, he had selected many beautiful tea sets.

But Suraj looked not very happy, he was quite.

Jin looked at him then asked: "Are you tired, Raj?"

Suraj looked at her eyes, didn't answer.

After ten minutes raining, the group moved again. They went to Jinli Ancient Street for shopping, and every body got some good stuff there.

In the evening, Jin took her tour group came to the most famous restaurant in Chengdu—Huang Cheng Lao Ma Hot Pot Buffet.

Suraj looked at the hot pot and so many foods on the conveyor belt, thinking: It's so hard to be a vegetarian. But Jin sisters and children were still eating vegetable only, even no spicy. Suraj shook head again, what should he do if he married a vegetarian?

The 6th day: to visit Chengdu Panda Breeding Base. Every body were so happy to see these cute baby pandas and enjoyed the big beautiful bamboo garden, it was also the first time they saw peacock, black swan and so many big gold fishes in the lake, they took a lots of pictures and bought some panda souvenirs.

Here was also the Key of Laboratory for Conservation Biology of Endangered Wildlife, Postdoctoral Programmer and Research Center.

The 7th day: they took Sichuan CYTS tour bus, traveled to Leshan, visit Leshan Giant Buddha.

"The mountain is a Buddha, the Buddha is a mountain". Leshan Giant Buddha Located in Leshan City, Sichuan Province, Leshan Giant Buddha was carved at the Mt. Lingyun rock walls Where is the place of three river confluence, it was the world's largest Maitreya Buddha carved statue. Leshan Giant Buddha's head as high as the mountain, feet were on the river, his hands were laying on the knees, sitting on riverside, body was 71 meters high, head is 14.7 meters high, 10 meters wide, ears were 7 meters long, nose was 5.6 meters long, eyes and mouth 3.3 m long, Shoulder was 24 m wide, finger was 8.3 meters length, from the knee to the instep 28 meters long, instep was 8.5 meters wide, more than a hundred people could sit on the foot.

Along the river cliff of Grand Buddha left and right sides, there were two warrior stone carved statues, tall more than 10 meters, handheld halberd, and thousands of statues of the rock carvings, stone carvings, to form a large group of Buddhist stone art.

Min River, Qingyi River and Dadu River aggregated at the Mt. Lingyun, ancient Leshan, the place of convergence of three rivers, the water was quite ferocious, boats were often subverted when came here. Whenever the summer flood season, the river destroyed the mountain, often causing the ship to crash tragedy. The monk Haitong saw this, determined to excavate Grand Buddha, to rely on Buddha's endless mana, made storm waves easy for the safe flow, to slow down the water potential, Monk Haitong went throughout the north and south of Long River to collect alms money for excavation Grand Buddha. After construction started, an local official came to extort funding, Haitong sternly rejected said: "I can dig out my eye, but you can not take Buddha's property." The local official bullying, Haitong really dug out his eye, holding the disk to show him, the official shocked, run away to regret.

Grand Buddha statues was carved in the Emperor Xuan Dynasty Tang, AD 713, after Haitong past away, Haitong's disciples took over the construction, completed in AD 803 and was through the efforts of three generations of artisans, which lasted 90 years.

In December 1996, Leshan Giant Buddha was approved by the UNESCO as the World Cultural and Natural Heritage.

When the tour guide led them walked up the mountain alone the stone step, Suraj saw many rock carvings on the cliffs on his left, but he didn't pay attention about these too much, he had been appreciating the scenery of three rivers on his right side. When he was passing a red rock carvings, he suddenly remembered something and looked back, four big characters on the rock walls "回头是岸"(Look back, the shore is right behind you.)

That night, they lived in Mt. Emei, campfire dinner with song and dance, and watched Sichuan Face-Changing show.

The 8th day: Emei Mount

Emei Mount, the most beautiful mountain in the world, known as China's four major Buddhist mountains, was a world famous temples Samantabhadra Bodhisattva. Emei Mount Wan Fo Ding peak elevation of 3079.3 meters. The whole situation and towering majestic mountains, rich vegetation, verdant vegetation, a considerable height, size large, thousands of miles to the very top overlooking the sea of clouds, in the golden dome can enjoy "sunrise", "sea of clouds", "Buddha" and "holy lights" four absolutely King. Mount Emei Buddha was the most magnificent spectacle. A total of dozens of Buddhist temples on Mount Emei, there were many fine collection of Buddhist treasures in the temples. Many elderly people endured the hardship devout Buddhist, stepped a break, after 10 days to reach the Peak. Searching for a myriad of tourists were attracted across the oceans, after several twists and turns, over several years beginning from the Hill was willing to cozy. Emei beautiful natural scenery, a good environment to make it become the base for exploring spot, monastic ideal of the premises.

In 1996, Mount Emei and the Leshan Giant Buddha together were included in the "World Natural and Cultural Heritage" and a dual natural and cultural heritage of all mankind.

When the group reached Wangnian Temple, it started to raining. Suraj shared a umbrella with Jin, she was their tour guide and translator, Suraj had to follow her all the time. Jin saw a linden three, she said to Suraj in German:

"When I went to University in Berlin, I often went to walk on the Unter Den Linden. I like there."

Suraj nodded, held umbrella, didn't say anything, kissed Jin on her forehead.

All tourists like Emei Trimeresurus Tea and Emei monkeys, they feed food to monkeys, but Medie said:

"These monkeys ate too much, get too fat, it's no good for them."

Every body laughed, but Suraj had been silent.

"Raj," Jin took his arm, "Take deep breath, relax yourself. Green plant cover 99% of the mountain, it just likes a huge oxygen bar here."

Suraj smiled, said: "Yes, angel."

Girls also tried to make Suraj smile.

"Uncle Raj, did you see the movie <<Kong Fu Panda>>?"

"Yes, I did, sweetie."

"We think the background of the movie was right here. Look at the high stairs."

"Oh, yah." Suraj nodded and smiled.

On the way to climb mountain, they heard a local man sang folk songs, and everybody laughed. Suraj asked Jin:

"What's that man singing?"

Ark answered him for Jin: "He's singing 'Build a temple on the hill, still feel low; sitting face to face, still miss you.'"

Suraj smiled, shook head.

Finally they reached the Gold Top of Mt. Emei. The rain stopped now. They saw 48-meter-high four sides Samantabhadra Buddha statue was sitting on a lotus throne and the Golden Elephant base.

"Wow—it's great!" Girls shouted.

Every body looked around then came into the souvenir store, Jin bought a gift for Suraj—a string of prayer beads, made of the seed of linden.

When everybody took pictures, Jin and Suraj stood by stone fence, looked at the sea of clouds under their feet. Heaven and earth was such a broad, time and space integrate.

"It's so beautiful!" Suraj said with a bit agitated, "Beautiful beyond my imagination. I've never been to such a mountain so high and so marvelous." He embraced Jin's shoulder, could not help having kissed her forehead.

"Thank you angel for bring me here."

"I'm happy too." Jin smiled, still looked at the sea of immense clouds, "Raj, do you hear the song of music?" She asked.

Suraj nodded: "Yes, angel, it's from your heart, you and your heart integrate with the time and the space."

"Yes. Music is harmony, all things harmonious, all things choral. You see—sun, moon, stars, clouds, mountains, thunder, lightning, rain, oceans, rivers, all trees, flowers, each leaf, every path, every elf, all birds, beasts, fishes and insects, all human beings, all gods, all of God's creation—every thing in the universe is going to be harmonious under God's baton . . . ." Jin smiled, "Unfortunately, this time we did not see the rainbow."

"Rainbow?" Suraj smiled too, "Nothing is perfect." Jin looked at him, then turned away to look at the Buddha statues. Suraj found that Jin's face gradually appeared a wonderful look, then he heard she said:

"Yes, it's perfect."

At the same moment, Suraj also heard thousands of people behind he were shouting, what was happened? He turned around to have a look, he was shocked immediately by the majestic scene in front of him—In the air, around Buddha Statue, two circular rainbow was appearing.

"Oh, God!"

And then, they heard the song of angels:

Somewhere over the rainbow way up high
There's a land that I heard of Once in a lullaby
Somewhere over the rainbow skies are blue
And the dreams that you dare to dream
Really do come true
Some day I'll wish upon a star
And wake up where the clouds are far behind me
Where troubles melt like lemon drops
Away above the chimney tops
That's where you'll find me

Somewhere over the rainbow
Bluebirds fly
Birds fly over the rainbow
Why then, oh why can't I?
Some day I'll wish upon a star
And wake up where the clouds are far behind me
Where troubles melt like lemon drops
Away above the chimney tops
That's where you'll find me
Somewhere over the rainbow
Bluebirds fly
Birds fly over the rainbow
Why then, oh why can't I?
If happy little bluebirds fly
Beyond the rainbow
Why, oh why can't I?

The 9th day: They went to visit Dujiangyan and Qingcheng Mountain. Along the way, they witnessed the debris after earthquake, many people lost their homes, still living in government-provided flat roof house. Jin's six kids were crying. Medie said to three foreign friends:

"Here is the hometown of five girls, they lost family and school in earthquake, the hometown of Ark was also in Sichuan, the village He had lived in was all submerged in mudslides, he was the only one alive."

The last evening in Chengdu, Jin took everybody came to Lao Shui Xing Restaurant, it was a famous Dum Sim tea house in Chengdu.

11

The 10th day: They checked out from hotel, took high speed electrified train for two hours to the next stop—Chongqing City.

Rosalyn said, she had not taken train for long time, this train was so fast, safe, clean and beautiful, more comfortable than airplane. Girls sang songs on the way, only Suraj looked not happy.

"Is Mr. Ram sick?" Kids asked.

"I don't think so." Rosalyn said.

"Yes, he is." Riccardo said, and smiled.

"Hi, uncle Raj, the sea of suffering is boundless, head back is the shore." Kids were joking with him.

Jin squeezed eyes to them, kids laughed, then quiet again.

At dusk, the tour group boarded on Victoria four-star luxury cruise ship "Archangel" from pier Chaotianmen, leaving Chongqing, started Three Gorges trip of three days.

Suraj and Ark shared a standard room, but Suraj didn't come to dinning room for dinner with every body, Ark said to Jin that Suraj was really got sick, his had head-ache, and vomiting. Jin immediately called a Chinese medicine on board came to Suraj's room.

Suraj was lying in the bed, feeling weak. Chinese medicine said that he got stomach flu. Jin asked kitchen to cooked some millet congee for Suraj, she feed him congee and the drug, then asked him to sleep.

At middle night, Suraj heard a soft music, he woke up, saw Jin was sitting on the other bed in meditation posture, eyes were closed, hands put on the knees, her lap top was on the bed by her, Suraj's keyboard was stood by her bed, and playing the music. Suraj knew that Jin was working, she was composing. He looked at her, she was so beautiful in the soft music, Suraj had never heard this music, made him feel in the mysterious forest, navigating in water, he heard the sound of cloud flying, the sound of water droplets in a cave, he heard the whispers of the universe, quiet, broad, far-reaching, flowing. At this moment, he saw Jin's hand moved, gently, follow the music, she started to conduct, very slow and soft. "It's so fantastic, angel, it's the music of fairy." Suraj said softly, closed his eyes.

Jin smiled then asked him softly: "I'm happy if you like it."

"The music beautiful like this, can heal all injured heart, comfort all tired body." Said Suraj.

"Thank you darling, I do hope so." Jin opened eyes, smiled and looked at Suraj, "I call it is Meditation Music. I am composing."

Suraj looked at her, smiled.

"Do you feel better now?" Jin came over by Suraj's bed, put hand on his forehead, and tried his body temperature, then she put three fingers on Suraj's wrist to take his pulse.

Suraj looked at her eyes, she was feeling his life with her life. This intimate touch made Suraj palpitates quickly, he said: "You always make me hot, angel."

Jin looked at him with smile, and whispered: "Not me, it's yourself, you make yourself hot. "She let go of his wrist, said, "You are getting better now, but still need more rest."

"I feel so sorry for the sickness on our trip, angel, I gave you so much trouble."

Jin smiled, said: "You should be hungry now." Suraj nodded.

Jin then got up to take millet soup for him.

"I asked the cook made for you, it has been stored in the insulation box."

"How could I thank you? Angel." Suraj looked at her.

Jin smiled: "Your stomach is still weak when without millet congee."

Suraj smiled, asked her: "How come they have millet on the cruise ship?"

Jin said that was she brought for him, just for in case.

Suraj looked at Jin, then closed eyes, said: "Angel."

"You really should love your body, respect the body, to be grateful to your body. The body is the visible soul, and the soul is invisible body. In your body is the water of the oceans, the fire of the stars and suns, in your body is the air, your God is right living in your body. Man is part of nature; his health is nothing but being in harmony with nature."

Jin helped him sat up, against the pillow. Suraj prayed and gave thanks before he ate the congee.

At this time, Peter and Rosalyn were in the bar, Rosalyn asked him:

"You say, honey, what reason can stop a man to love a woman?"

"You mean Suaj?

"Ehn hen."

"I think, may be because of the religious reason, Suraj is a Christian, his family are Christians, he should marry a Christian wife. But Jin is not a Christian, she studies Holy Bible, she takes her kids to Church, but she studies Buddhist and Taoist too. What should Suraj do?"

"But he can change, or he can change Jin."

"Do you think Jin will be changed by Suaj?"

Rosalyn shrugged shoulders and drank: "It's hard for them. You see, Jin has so many kids already, so busy, I don't think she will have time to make her own babies, that's a problem for her marriage. Unless, a man loves her and no matter about this."

Peter Riccardo nodded.

"So, what's the matter any way? Why Suraj could not tell Jin he loves her?"

"Maybe, "Peter said, "perhaps he has a girlfriend already."

Rosalyn looked at Peter: "Oh, come on! We had never heard about this?!"

Peter shrugged shoulders and drank the red wine: "Who knows? He doesn't like to talk. God knows. Everyone has his own secret."

Rosalyn shrugged shoulders, sighted: "Any way, Raj is not happy, every body can see, but no body can help, he fell in love with Jin, period, but, there is a enormous barrier between them . . . ."

"He fell in the sea of suffering, head back is the shore." Peter said, and smiled.

The 11th day. In morning, the cruise ship arrived in the Fengdu Ghost City, "Oriental Divine Comedy hometown", also called the Nether World.

Two hundreds tourists, more than one hundred came from U.K. every body followed the tour guide disembark landing to visit. But Suraj Ram was still weak. Jin asked him to stay in the room, and she would stay with him.

"Don't worry," She said. "I've been here before." Jin turned on her laptop, started working. Suraj asked what she was doing, Jin said that she was composing meditation music, the name of this album called ZEN SPA. She showed Suraj some sheets witch she has written. Suraj read it, and immediately got up to turn on his keyboard.

Jin used a variety of Chinese and Western musical instruments in these songs, especially the flute, zither, hulusi and chimes, Suraj particularly like the sound of water droplets in caves.

"So beautiful!" he said," just like you."

In the afternoon, they sat on the sun boat board, enjoy the sunshine and breeze, the picturesque beauty of the Three Gorges.

"It's really beautiful, China." Rosalyn was talking with Suraj, Peter was drinking beer with a British old gentleman. Then they saw the Hanging Coffins: The Ba people that dwelled here thousands of years ago had the custom of putting coffins in to the cliff crevices high above the river. It was said to be a unique way of burying the rich. Suraj looked at those coffins, said: "I like this way, it's much better than we are lying under the ground."

"Yah, that's right." Rosalyn said, "who like to live in basement? Every body wants to live higher, like this, more air, also can see beautiful view. It's really a good idea."

Riccardo laughed when he heard this, said: "Why you guys don't want to live in heaven but on the cliff?"

After dinner, many people went to the party room to dance, Jin took kids back to the cabin to rehearse. Suraj stayed in his room alone again, he started to play Jin's Zen Spa Music, and missed her, the music sooner comfort his heart.

"She's a great musician," he thought, "and an sweet angel. But she is not a Christian. Tell me please what should I do? God, I love her!" Suraj prayed for a long time this night before he head to bed.

An other day: Cruise arrived at Xiling Gorge, the morning tour was to Baidicheng, afternoon tour was Shennongxi.

Jin, Medie and kids got up early, when there was no one came to the sun board on the top of the ship, Jin, Medie and kids started to play Tai Chi sword. Suraj came out to find them, he took video for them, it would be never enough to him to watch Jin. Sooner, more people came to board, some of them followed the girls to play Tai Chi, even some foreigners. What a beautiful landscapes in the dawn it is.

Baidicheng, was built in late West Han Dynasty. Distinguished for its lasting literary works left by ancient poets and scholars, such as Li Bai, Du Fu, it was also honored as Town of Poem.

Jin explained Li Bai's poem to them:" The apes on the both side of the river keep to cry, the light boat has past ten thousand mountains."

Qu Yuan Temple.

"Raj do you remember you ate Zong Zi with us in Dragon Boat Festival?" Jin asked.

"Yes I do, angel." Suraj thought of two months ago, he went to Chinese supermarket T $ T in Toronto with Jin, there were a variety of flavors Zong there, chicken flavor Zong, mushrooms Zong, curry beef Zong, seafood Zong, date and peanuts Zong, Taiwan salty meat Zong, Japanese red bean Zong, Malaysia Nyonya Zong, Vietnamese banana in coconut cream Zong . . . . that day Suraj ate too much Zong Zi, then got stomach pain.

"Did I tell you the origins of Zong?" Jin asked again. Suraj shook head.

"Ok, in the year of 340 BC, the Chu patriotic poet Qu Yuan could not faces the pain of subjugation, in the fifth month, bitterly jumped into river. Because he was so patriotic, people loved him, didn't want fished damage his body, so they installed bamboo rice into the river, let fishes to eat. Later, in order to express the reverence and nostalgia of Qu Yuan, in annual Dragon Boat Festival, people would make bamboo leaves rice, homage on the river, even in Toronto, every year in June, you can see the dragon boat races."

That day at night, Suraj stayed on the top board with Jin. The sky was already dark, but still could see the mountains on the both side of the river. It was the good time to see stars, and all the constellations were so close, big, seems could reach them by hands. Quiet, wide, air from the universe, with infinite clarity of magnetic energy, Their whole body felt was melting in Heaven, they sat in meditation, felt like they were driving the ship in the universe.

Three Gorges Dam, the largest water conservancy project in the world with total storage capacity of 39.3 billion cubic meters and annual generating capacity of 84 kilowatts, the dam is 2335 meters long, 185 meters high. For the construction of the Three Gorges Dam, raising the water level, and submerged 20 cities, 277 towns, 1,680 villages, more than one million of people immigrated.

In the afternoon, they got off the ship, went to the Three Gorges Airport. At dusk, they came back to Beijing.

Had to say Bye to family and China again.

"There still are many beautiful places we didn't go, such as Huangshan Mount, Taishan Mount, Wudang Mount, and Guilin, Suzhou, Tibet, Hong Kong . . . . but we don't have more time. Leave for the next trip." Said Medie.

"When will be the next time?" kids asked.

"Well, we has received the invitation of the National Theatre, will be back in this Christmas and New Year for performances, mom Jin will conduct National Opera Ballet of theater and Hong Kong Pan Asia Symphony Orchestra, held two symphonic chorus concerts."

Suraj was still in silence.

"What are you thinking? Raj." Jin calmly asked him.

"I am thinking about that question you have left to me. I am thinking about where is my shore."

"The shore sometimes is only a balance beam;" Jin said, "some times, it's a ark; sometimes, we lost the shore, even don't have an ark, don't have a piece of wood; In this time, what can we do? In the boundless suffering sea, who will raise us up to walk on the stormy sea? Who will raise us up, so we can stand on mountains? Love is the shore, faith is the shore. If music was able to connect all the shores, all the souls, all things in the world would be in harmonic."

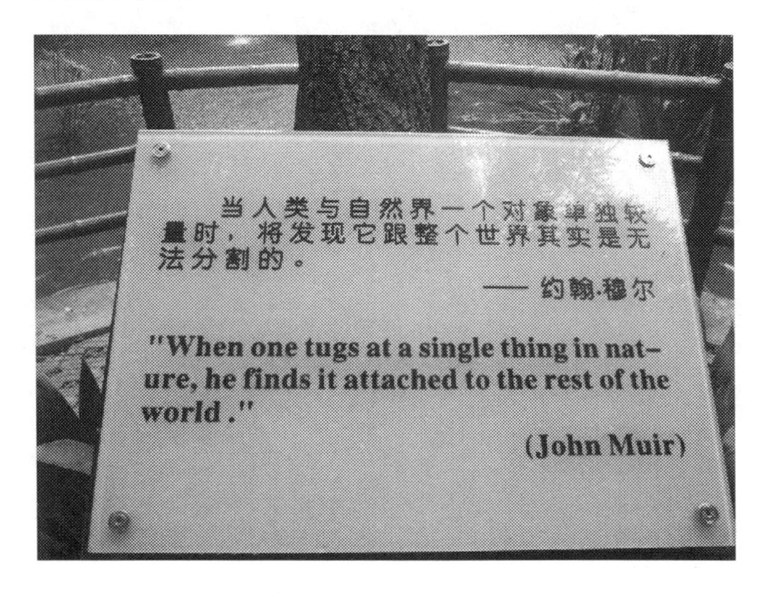
当人类与自然界一个对象单独较
量时，将发现它跟整个世界其实是无
法分割的。
—— 约翰·穆尔
"When one tugs at a single thing in nature, he finds it attached to the rest of the
world ."
(John Muir)

—The End—

Anne Wien Lynn

Thanksgiving Day in 2012 in Toronto